THE BLIND SEARCH

THE BLIND
SEARCH

LESLEY EGAN

PUBLISHED FOR THE CRIME CLUB BY

DOUBLEDAY & COMPANY, INC.

GARDEN CITY, NEW YORK

1977

All of the characters in this book
are fictitious, and any resemblance
to actual persons, living or dead,
is purely coincidental.

First Edition

ISBN: 0-385-12356-6
Library of Congress Catalog Card Number 76–23774
Copyright © 1977 by Elizabeth Linington
All Rights Reserved
Printed in the United States of America

It takes two to speak the truth—one to speak and another to hear.

—HENRY DAVID THOREAU

THE BLIND SEARCH

ONE

"At least," said Jesse, "you can go back to bed."

"Me and Athelstane," agreed Nell, finishing her coffee. "I know I once said two at least, but right now I'll settle for the one we've got." She yawned.

Jesse grinned at her. "Old Hebrew proverb—small children disturb one's sleep, big children one's life."

"Don't borrow trouble," said Nell sleepily. David Andrew, aged five months, had kept them up most of the night; she was still in her robe, her waist-length brown hair untidily braided. Athelstane, the mastiff, who was a conscientious dog, had dutifully patrolled the nursery too, and now was dozing heavily on Jesse's feet. Jesse prodded him.

"Get off me, monster—I've got to go to work."

"And do have a nice day." Nell yawned again. The baby, of course, was now peacefully asleep. "Don't forget Fran and Andrew are coming for dinner." As Jesse got up she poured herself more coffee.

Switching on the ignition and backing the Dodge out into the drive, Jesse shook himself further awake with a little effort, and it wasn't only the effect of one sleepless night. He felt stale and slightly jaundiced with life; maybe along in the mid-thirties most people did, with the dawning realization that it seemed to be just more of the same damned thing over and over.

Even after three months he had to remind himself not to turn left on Hollywood Boulevard; he went straight down to Wilshire, lucky in missing signals. He'd moved into the new office in May—just before the old man went. It was a bigger, newer office in a tall building out on Wilshire, with a more spacious waiting room, a secretarial office big enough to accommodate all his growing files and his new and invaluable twin secretaries; business had picked up over the last couple of years, and in a few other ways he'd been lucky. But, having left the Dodge in the basement garage and ridden the elevator up to the third floor, he wandered down the carpeted corridor to regard his office door with something near to dislike.

The sign was new too, conforming to all the other signs on doors here in shape, finish and lettering. J. D. FALKENSTEIN, ATTORNEY-AT-LAW.

He went in, and routine snapped him up with its inaudible jaws. "Morning, girls."

The Gordons, Jean and Jimmy (Jamesina) looked up smiling from typewriter and filing cabinet. Nice girls: efficient and pretty, and nearly identical: natural blonds with big brown eyes. "Good morning, Mr. Falkenstein—" Jean; "I'll have the Dixon will ready this morning. Mr. Blythe just called, he wants to see you at one to discuss the Acme suit."

"Oh, hell," said Jesse.

"And the Reddin divorce hearing's been postponed again," said Jimmy. "I don't know what these judges do to earn their salaries, every time they feel like a day off— You've got an appointment at ten, new clients, and the Frommer-Dakin contract's on your desk, I finished typing it last night."

"I don't know why I bother to come in," said Jesse. "You girls could run the place between you." He went on into his office, sat at the desk and absently pulled his tie loose; the neat blue-covered package of the contract was centered on the blotter, but he didn't pick it up. Air conditioning on in here; it was August and a heat wave building up outside. He looked around the good-sized square room, vaguely dissatisfied with himself and life.

A nice office, prosperous-looking. Nell had picked out the moss-green carpet, the bleached oak paneling. The L-shaped desk still felt too big after the years at his old one. The silent-gliding file drawers at one side were convenient, the tape recorder discreetly mounted underneath. Facing him on the opposite wall was the one picture, a commandingly large and good print, heavily walnut-framed, of Holbein's portrait of Sir Thomas More. Surprisingly, that had been the old man's gift. The thin ascetic face with its long Norman nose, faint shadow of beard and brilliant dark eyes seemed to stare back at him remotely.

"Oh, hell," he said to himself again, and reached reluctantly for the contract. He heard the outer door open and shut: the mail, probably. *Whereas the party of the first part, subject to the exceptions noted below, agrees . . .*

"Am I interrupting anything?"

Match poised to a cigarette, Jesse glanced up and after a moment said, "Come in," and jumped and swore as the match flame reached his finger.

"Seen a ghost?" said his visitor, dead-pan.

"Something like that." Jesse lit the cigarette and leaned back. How many times did the old man look in just like that and say the same thing— Never mind. "What are you doing here, William?"

"Got something to show you," said DeWitt laconically. "I don't know if you'll think it's worth interrupting your torts or whatever." He sat down in one of the clients' chairs, a man nearly as lank and tall and dark as Jesse, his thin intelligent face impassive, and took off his black-rimmed glasses; he made no move to open the brief case on his knees.

Jesse cocked his head at him. "Something?"

"Not much," said DeWitt. "It's so much like groping in the dark. Blindman's buff. I just thought you'd like to see it." He began to open the brief case.

Jesse put down the contract. Sudden and fleeting, he was thinking of the day DeWitt had showed up here so unexpectedly, last May. Sitting where he sat now, talking and talking, bitter, resigned, humorous, cynical, hopeful, dogged. He thought now, a little cynical himself on that, that it could possibly be that whatever else he'd accomplished or would accomplish in life might turn out to be less important than his tenuous association with DeWitt. Or, of course, possibly not.

What came out of the brief case was a tightly rolled scroll of ordinary cheap drawing paper. "Mrs. Ventnor," said Jesse with a small sigh.

"Well, in the midst of all the chaff—"

"Good term for it. The automatic writing I suspect just congenitally."

He'd first met DeWitt a couple of years ago when a client of his had got herself murdered. Margaret Brandon, a nice woman: and a privately practicing trance medium. It was that small association that had set Jesse to reading some in the field. DeWitt had been on the staff of the Parapsychology Foundation at the time; after he'd been back to testify at the trial, Jesse hadn't seen or heard of him until that day last May. He'd been a dispirited man, and he'd unburdened himself to Jesse, as an interested layman who had a sufficient background of knowledge in the subject but wasn't officially associated with it.

"I swear to God," he said, "the whole parcel of them are as much slaves to orthodoxy as those fellows who took after Galileo. I have had it, Falkenstein. Going around in circles—and not even coming full circle back to where it started, at that. I'd be the first to admit that, at least for now, we can't call psychic research an exact science, but if we're going to use the scientific method at it, there are certain first principles, for God's sake. All right—all right! It seems to me, just speaking as a damn fool who's spent twenty-five years studying the subject, that the one unequivocal first principle here is the question of individual survival of death. Everything else, for God's sake, grows out of that, all the rest of it is—side roads. Whatever fancy names they dream up for all the rest—telepathy, telekinesis, teleportation, apports, whatever the hell psychic forces—it's all of a piece, and the one central important fact, the significant evidence underlying all of it, is the evidence for individual survival."

"You sound like one of those impassioned spiritualists, circa 1890."

"My God, do I know it!" yelped DeWitt. "Don't tell me—you've read some of that, you said, all the evidence we've already got. Reams of it, all buried in the musty old files of the British and American societies, and who the hell has read it in the last fifty years? Of the stuff that got into public print, reams of that too, who the hell reads Myers and Sidgwick and Lodge and Doyle these days?"

"Your foundation—"

"Not mine. I have had it with all these people—not just the foundation, but every so-called research organization I know of—part of it is that they're following fashion, I suppose you could say, but the upshot is that they've all thrown out the baby with the bath, and don't mention mixed metaphors to me. Wasting time and money and argument over card-guessing games and mental marvels who can bend picture wire by concentration, and they won't touch the survival evidence with a barge pole. They're so damned determined to be accepted as scientists with a capital, they shy off that like—like scared sheep," said DeWitt. "Short-sighted—or do I mean blind? Do they think, my God, they can escape the one central fact by just not talking about it? If you postulate a psychic force at all, damn what forms it takes, from poltergeists to clairvoyance to telekinesis, the ultimate conclusion comes right back to personal survival, the persisting soul, and once you've got sound evidence for that everything else follows. I tell you," said DeWitt angrily, "I'm beginning to believe, absurd as it sounds to anyone who knows the literature, that we've got to go right back to the start, produce all the evidence all over again for this century. This damned skeptical materialistic century that can't believe those old fellows back in the eighties and nineties were capable of using scientific methods. Maybe if we rubbed their noses in it— And there've been hints of a couple of new exciting things in that direction, if some concerted effort was made to follow it up in an organized way—the tape communication, if you—"

"That," said Jesse, "is but too far out."

"Not that far. It opens such possibilities— Bayliss has suggested, and I'm bound to say it strikes me as damned logical, that one reason this century hasn't got even the handful of really great mediums the nineteenth had is that the other side is tired of trying to use the imperfect human personality—even with a good medium the unconscious is always interfering—and possibly the various technical experts on that plane want to experiment—"

"Don't like that word 'planes.' Call it levels of vibration."

"—experiment with machines instead. It makes some sort of sense. But damn the vehicle, it seems to me we've got to go right back to the beginning and collect the same sort of solid survival evidence all over again—not to get the scientific recognition, my God, but to open any new paths for investigation at all. Stop fooling around on all the side roads, and get back to solid research. What I'm proposing is something on the lines of the British mediums' bureau, a small set fee for sittings with mediums, and full records kept. As the evidence accumulates, get it in print—"

"What impression do you think you might make? I see what you're getting at, but trying to break the barriers of orthodox science, when the Rhines and your foundation are just barely respectable even now—"

"Barely! Barriers and orthodox science be damned," said DeWitt roundly. "To get even the bare recognition, they've chased off down all the side roads—scared of the four-letter word *soul*."

"And I don't know that it'd do much for my reputation to be associated with you, if you were asking."

DeWitt laughed. "You don't have to appear on a letterhead. But a few of us are getting together on it, and we'll need a treasurer to keep a few accounts. I suppose we could manage a fee. Knowing you're interested in the field—"

And that had been the week after the old man died. Jesse had said abruptly, surprising himself, "I might waive the fee, DeWitt, if you could get me a bona-fide communication. . . ."

Old Edgar Walters had been a friend for only those few short years, and he'd had a good-sized family of his own, and, Jesse supposed, an eminently satisfactory life—and death, for he'd gone the way he'd have chosen, the old reprobate: between one second and another, as he renewed a third drink from the bottle always bulging his jacket. Eighty-four his last birthday, and still as shrewd as they came, still forever interested in life and people: it was reasonable to suppose that he still was, and still concerned with the people who'd meant something to him here—planes or levels of vibrations or whatever. It seemed that he'd thought something of Jesse Falkenstein; he'd left him a lot of money in a new will. The old man had had a lot of money to leave, and most of it had gone to his family, all of whom were nice respectable people with better sense than to waste it on an attempt to contest the will. It had been a surprise to Jesse; but he'd rather have had the old man still around, looking in his office door—"Not interruptin' anything important, hey?"—and on occasion coming out with some shrewd piece of advice over a puzzle.

DeWitt's little organization now had a name—the Western Association for Psychic Research—and a letterhead, and modest quarters in a rather shabby office out on Santa Monica Boulevard, and records were starting to fill its filing cabinets, for what they were worth. A couple of local members of the foundation, Marcus Golding and Arthur Haney, both with enough money to spare, had underwritten the fairly modest upkeep. DeWitt wasn't dependent on a salary, had private means of his own. They had come up with four "developing psychics," as the term was these days, willing and eager to dedicate their time for the small set fees, the sittings by appointment presided over by DeWitt's inhumanly efficient secretary, Miss Duffy. Mrs. Alice Ventnor produced the automatic writing; Cora Delaney and Wanda Moreno were trance mediums, and Charles MacDonald had some reputation as a psychometrist.

Now and then Jesse dropped in to look at the latest transcriptions, or DeWitt brought him some interesting tidbit that had just showed up. DeWitt was a happy man, pottering about his chosen piece of research; that it was difficult and obscure ground to work he had already known.

Now Jesse looked at the long scroll of drawing paper in DeWitt's hand with faint cynicism and repeated, "Mrs. Ventnor."

"Well, we have to take what comes," said DeWitt. "There's always a good deal of chaff in automatic writing. You have to sort out the few grains of wheat there may be. I just thought you'd like to see this, for whatever it's worth. It came through last night." He began to unroll the scroll, and Jesse reached for the bottom of it, only faintly interested.

It was a very typical example of automatic writing: covered all over with penciled scrawls, exhibiting at least eight different scripts from a childishly large half-printing to a fine, near-Spencerian hand. It was, of course, shirking the accumulated evidence to put all automatic writing down as a product of the unconscious mind, but it wasn't the kind of evidence Jesse liked; it was chancy, scrambled.

He didn't like this example of it much at all. As usual, it consisted of a lot of disconnected words and half sentences without capitals or punctuation. *Claire clare de lune i didnt want to go meet me you met me i wanted want you to listen when i try—* The lines trailed off the right side of the page, the script changed, more disconnected words not making much sense, a beautiful series of precise circles, more jumbled phrases in the Spencerian hand.

Jesse grunted at it. "There may be something there," said DeWitt,
"all that Claire bit. It seems to be part of a longer attempt at communication, some of it's come through Mrs. Delaney in trance, but
we haven't correlated it all yet. This is what I wanted you to see."
His long forefinger pointed out a single line in the center of the
page.

It was in an angular, square script, heavy and firm: the single in-
stance of that on the page. *will try will will try now tell j j j j will try*
wait and see get thru.

Jesse shook his head at it. "It might mean anything."

DeWitt began to roll up the scroll again. "It might. But whoever,
whatever produces all that, it is communication, you know. From
mind to mind—one entity invisible to us, but there. Wherever. In-
controvertibly there." He put the scroll away in his brief case and
gave Jesse a sudden open grin. "I suspect, you hardheaded shyster,
that you sometimes think we're all wasting our lives chasing after
fairy gold. But it's worth doing, as it was worth doing nearly a hundred years back when those first researchers blazed the trail." He fas-
tened the brief case slowly. "In the furor and madness and blood
that is the twentieth century we've got to believe that it's worth
doing."

Jean Gordon's neat blond head poked in the door. "Mr. and Mrs.
Lanning are here, Mr. Falkenstein."

"I'm just going," said DeWitt.

Jesse put out his cigarette and stood up automatically. The Lannings were new clients.

They came in purposefully, and trouble came with them, he saw.
Trouble often came in with clients to a lawyer's office. He sized
them up at a glance: no money to guess at, but nice people, both in
their forties, well-dressed if not smart. Lanning was stocky, a little
overweight, his sandy hair receding from a high forehead; he wore
rimless glasses, a decent gray suit with a white shirt and discreet tie.
She had probably been a pretty girl and was still attractive, with a
trim figure, her dark hair simply waved back from a round face. She

wore glasses too, and not much makeup; her plain blue voile summer dress was crisply pressed. She's been crying and he looked depressed.

"Mr. Falkenstein," he said in an unexpected bass voice, and offered a soft hand. "We heard—that is, you were recommended to us by Mrs. Basehart."

"Oh, yes," said Jesse. That damage suit—details came back to him —the Basehart woman, a teacher, honest, forthright, co-operative. "Sit down, won't you? What can I do for you?"

They sat down side by side in the clients' chairs. Mrs. Lanning set her white patent-leather handbag on her knees and clasped it tightly. Her nails were uncolored; she wore a wedding ring only. She looked at her husband, and then she said to Jesse, "There's so much to— we'd better not both try. Fred, you just tell him all of it, from the beginning."

"So you'll have all the background." Lanning nodded. "I'll just say, I don't know what you can do for us—maybe not much—but we thought we'd better try, anyway. First I'd better tell you something about ourselves. We're both teachers, Mr. Falkenstein. At a private school—the Christian Church Academy, it's a small school—elementary through junior high—connected with our church. It's just on the edge of the Atwater district, Dover Place, and we live on Kingsley in Hollywood. We own our home there. We—Susan and I've been married twenty-two years."

"Yes, Mr. Lanning." Jesse slid down in the desk chair and lit a cigarette, watching them.

"You probably know," said Lanning, "that that area is mixed residential. We have a single house, there are mostly single homes on our block, but across the street and down the next block there are apartment houses, four-family places, duplexes. I'm trying to think how to tell you all this the shortest way, not wasting your time—"

"Don't worry about that, Mr. Lanning. Just tell it your own way."

"We've never had any children, you see. We talked about adoption at one time, but there seemed to be so much red tape, and of course with Susan working too we couldn't take foster children. We're both fond of children, but I suppose you could say we had a—an outlet in the school, working closely with children as we do. I teach mathematics, history and Latin in the junior high school grades, and Susan teaches English and history in the lower grades. We both take a Sunday-school class." He had a clear precise manner of speech, and Jesse found himself thinking that he was probably a very good teacher.

"That's enough background," said Mrs. Lanning energetically. "You see, Mr. Falkenstein, this goes back nearly eight years—seven and a half—and there's so much to tell you. We—"

"I'm telling him, Sue."

"The reason Fred mentioned about the apartments, there's one up at the corner of Fountain a block away, and that's where she lived. Then. Nonie. Nonie Johnson. Seven and a half years ago, Josie was just sixteen months old. There, I'm sorry, Fred, I said just one of us had better do the talking. You go on."

"She was a very pretty girl, Nonie," he went on quietly, "only about nineteen. And alone. She told us she was married and her husband had left her. We never decided whether that was true or not— we never laid eyes on Josie's father. Nonie was working as a waitress somewhere, she left the baby at a day-care center, but sometimes when she wanted to go out in the evening, she'd ask us to baby-sit."

"It was only natural she should want to go out sometimes," broke in Mrs. Lanning, "a pretty girl like that, and as we said, if the baby was illegitimate at least she thought enough of her to keep her. Then. Not just put her out— And a lot of young girls aren't brought up to take care of a house, children, properly. In a way, it'd have been better if she had—"

"Susan," he said tiredly, "don't be charitable."

"I don't feel charitable, and I don't feel Christian about it!" she said fiercely, her mouth tight. "And I'm not ashamed of it either. That poor baby—we first got to know Nonie when she'd come by on the weekends, she hadn't a car and she went up to the market on Santa Monica to shop. The first time she asked us to baby-sit, honestly, Mr. Falkenstein, that poor mite was filthy. Such a darling baby, just not looked after. I don't know about the day-care center, some of them are all right, but it's not individual care. The poor child's clothes were practically in tatters and hadn't been washed in weeks, and—well, all right, Fred, I just wanted to explain. We felt sorry for her—I even felt sorry for Nonie then. She was young, and maybe she just didn't know how to take care of a baby. I tried to tell her this and that, in a nice way, you know. But later—because we baby-sat Josie quite a lot that next six or seven months—it was just the same—the dirty clothes, she only had two or three outfits, and half the time she hadn't been fed when Nonie brought her. And then she just left Josie with us and disappeared," said Mrs. Lanning baldly.

Jesse sat up. "Oh, she did. This was when?"

"I have all the dates and relevant information here," said Lanning, bringing out a manila envelope. He blinked short-sightedly at Jesse over it. "Not that I can think it'll be of much help, but that's why we've come to you—you'll know what the legal situation is. That was on September seventh, six years ago. That is, it will be six years next month. It was a Saturday night, and Nonie phoned to ask if we'd take care of Josie for the evening. She dropped her off at about eight o'clock, and that was the last we saw of her—Nonie—for some time."

"Exactly how much time?"

"Eight weeks. Naturally, when she didn't come to pick up the baby, we went to the apartment. She wasn't there, no one had seen her or knew where she was. Well, we were fond of the child by then, Josie that is—a very sweet-natured child, and a very bright one —and we just went on caring for her. We took her to the school with us during the week, she was really very good, and Mrs. Burns— our principal—was sympathetic. Then about two months later there was a note from Nonie. She said she was sorry to have left the baby so long but she'd suddenly got the offer of a good job in Las Vegas and she couldn't take care of the baby there, so would we keep her awhile longer. And she enclosed fifty dollars. In cash."

"Well, well," said Jesse. "And so you went on taking care of the baby."

"Yes, of course. To cut a long story short," said Lanning, "we've had Josie ever since. Six years. We've brought her up, Mr. Falkenstein. She's like our own—she calls us Daddy Fred and Mother Sue. She doesn't remember Nonie—didn't—she wasn't quite three when we first had her. Nonie's never been back to see her, or us. She never sent Josie Christmas presents or birthday presents. At intervals we've had a little money from her, nothing to speak of—twenty dollars, ten dollars, once seventy-five. But—"

"How much altogether?" asked Jesse. Lanning would know exactly.

"Two hundred and ten dollars, on five occasions over the first two years. There'd be a little note along with the money—I've got them all here," and he tapped the envelope. "Just, sorry I can't come for the baby yet, or, hope the baby's O.K. That was all."

"No addresses?"

"As you'll see, one was postmarked Las Vegas, and one she evidently wrote while she was staying with her mother—an address in Torrance. You'll wonder why we never tried to contact her—"

"No," said Jesse. "Don't rock the boat." He slid farther down in his chair.

"That was it!" cried Mrs. Lanning. "At first we said, well, at least Josie's being cared for properly—and then when she started Sunday school and kindergarten, and was doing so well—a good basic grounding, we concentrate on the old-fashioned three R's, you know, and Josie was always so quick at everything, a bright child. When we thought how she might have been raised—that girl racketing around heaven knows where or with what sort of characters—we felt, just, the longer we had her the better for Josie. But all the time—all the time—"

"Um, yes, sword of Damocles," said Jesse.

"Apt," said Lanning shortly. He took off his glasses and rubbed his forehead. "About two years ago we took legal advice. Susan said, if we could just quietly adopt her legally—I didn't think it would be possible, but we asked. A Mr. Pomeroy—he had an office on Fountain near our home. I'm bound to say neither of us cared for him much, he didn't seem interested, but I think he's a competent lawyer. He told us it couldn't be done. Even if the child was illegitimate, Nonie was her natural mother, and she had relatives who'd enter in the picture—her mother, and she'd mentioned a sister. We couldn't adopt Josie without informing Nonie, and at the time we didn't know where she was. We both thought there might be a chance that Nonie would agree—at that time—but we couldn't do anything about it."

"So you just went on the way you had been."

"We hadn't even heard from her in more than three years," said Mrs. Lanning. "The time she sent the seventy-five dollars was four years ago—all the money came in the first two years, and since then nothing. We had another note more than three years ago, and then nothing. She just said she hoped the baby was O.K. and sorry she couldn't send any money. You see, Mr. Falkenstein, by then we hoped we'd never hear anything again. That she'd just—"

"Mmh, yes. Forget about Josie altogether."

"But she had!" burst out Mrs. Lanning with a little sob. "She had —you can see that! Just walking off and leaving her! It wasn't as though she really knew us—we might have been anybody—she'd only seen us, walking by when we were out working in the front yard, saying hello, and wasn't it a nice day. We only agreed to baby-sit Josie those first times because we felt sorry for— And then she just went off and left her. She simply didn't care, she couldn't be bothered to take care of a child, it was just luck that Josie didn't end up in an orphanage, if we hadn't— But she's like our own, we've brought her up to be a nice child—a very bright girl, she's doing long division already and reading above her age level, of course she's always been a reader from the time she learned—and—" Quite suddenly Mrs. Lanning, who up to now had maintained a tight, controlled poise, dissolved in a flood of sobs. She put her neat dark head down on her handbag and gulped and wept.

"Ah, Sue," said Lanning sadly. "Sue." He took a handkerchief from his breast pocket, wiped his own eyes and looked at Jesse with the nakedly unfocused stare of the myopic. "We're taken up enough of your time, Mr. Falkenstein. I'd better tell you the rest and ask what you think we might do. If anything. As my wife says, it had been over three years since we'd heard from Nonie. Then last Saturday night we had a phone call. Just out of the blue. She said she wanted the baby back, she'd take the baby off our hands was how she put it. That she had a good job and could afford to take care of her now, and she'd come the next day to pick her up. I was so taken aback that I'm afraid I didn't—I couldn't—put up much of an argument. I started to try, but she simply hung up and that was that.

"Well, she came. Last Sunday morning about ten o'clock. My God," said Lanning not irreverently, "she looks so much older, harder—in just six years. I can't tell you"—he gestured helplessly at Jesse—"how it was. What—what could we say to Josie? We'd tried —overnight—but we couldn't know what would happen, how—how permanent—or what we could do. Josie—she didn't remember her real mother, the only home and parents she's known have been us, the school, a settled routine life. What could we say to her? She didn't want to go off with a strange woman, she begged us not to let the woman take her and what in God's name could we *do?*" Lanning shut his eyes. "That woman—it's hard to understand a woman like that—I think—it was as if she'd forgotten how much time had gone by, as if she'd left a baby with us and expected to find a baby still there. She just looked at Josie and said—using an obscenity—she didn't believe it. She was—"

"*Fulsome.* Then," said Mrs. Lanning, raising her head, "my own sweet little girl, aren't you glad to see Mama again? Of all the ridiculous things to—and Josie—Josie—she's such a reserved child, she just didn't understand any of it, why she had to go away from home with that woman—I'm sorry, Fred, you said I lost control of myself, I know I did, but I had to try! Don't you see, Mr. Falkenstein, I had to try—after she wouldn't listen to Fred! I tried to tell her—how Josie didn't remember her at all, she was like ours, all the time we'd had her—it wasn't fair—and we wanted to adopt her if only Nonie'd agree, wouldn't she please consider it—I know it was the wrong way to do it, it frightened Josie, but the woman was already just walking out pulling Josie along, and I had to— And Josie was crying, she never does cry, even the time she fell off the swing and broke her arm—the last time I saw Josie cry like that was when Laddie died— our old cocker, he was old when we first had Josie but they loved each other—and—and—*Bix!*" sobbed Sue Lanning, mopping her eyes. "I don't know what to do about Bix—our beagle that we got after Laddie—he and Josie just inseparable, he's moped around ever since and won't eat—and *where is she?* Where's Josie now? That woman took her away—she didn't give me a chance to pack all Josie's things, or any but a couple of her books, or— And we've tried the phone number a thousand times and nobody ever answers—"

"What can we do, Mr. Falkenstein?" asked Lanning. "Is there anything we can do legally?"

Jesse stabbed out his cigarette. "Not much, Mr. Lanning," he said sadly. "We can try. She left you a phone number where you could keep in touch?"

"I have never laid hands on a woman in my life, but if I'd had to

—I insisted. I tried to get it through her head—I never thought she was a very intelligent girl, and six years hasn't improved her—that she was a stranger to Josie, she was taking her away from home, we wanted to keep in touch, see Josie when we could—and she finally gave me a phone number. But we haven't raised an answer there yet."

"However, she did give it to you," said Jesse. "I'll tell you the worst of it right off. She is the legal mother. The evidence is that she made an effort to pay for the child's care. If inadequate. She kept in touch with you—though that gap of three years is something. Sporadically in touch. Legal inference, she didn't abandon the child. Legally, you haven't got a leg to stand on, any more than if you'd agreed to baby-sit the child and then refused to give her up."

"Thanks very much," said Lanning. Mrs. Lanning sat up, pale and tense, and stared at Jesse.

"On the other hand, strange as it may seem, the courts have now and then taken a realistic stand on this sort of case, just recently. Same like child labor laws—struck a lot of people as unreasonable that kids of seven or eight shouldn't go out to work a twelve-hour day like everybody else, they were reasonable human beings—then, with all the finicky laws in, seemed as if the courts reckoned they were soft-headed idiots until they got to be eighteen or twenty-one. Just lately there've been a number of cases here and there where a judge seemed to feel that a child of nine or ten could reasonably say whether he'd rather live with mama or papa, or even—in a few cases —with foster parents. I'm not going to tell you"—he stood up slowly, unfolding his lean length—"that this is going to be easy, or even possible, because we don't know. We don't, for example, know much about Nonie. Just from the little you've told me, possibly we could show she's an unfit mother. But even if a judge said so, Josie'd end up as a ward of the court, and there'd be a lot of red tape trying to apply as foster parents. But there are things we can try here. Just what you've said, Nonie sounds like a flitterbrain. Irresponsible. Kind that doesn't know what she wants. Small glimmer of a conscience, or she wouldn't have sent you that money. But conceivably, whyever she decided to take Josie back, she'll have had enough of taking care of a child in a little bit, and might be open to agree to your adopting her. That's the best that might be. I'd say—"

"Oh, but Josie's a good girl," said Mrs. Lanning. "A very quiet child—no trouble at all. But not to know where she is—and that terrible woman— But, oh, Mr. Falkenstein, she didn't really want her! I could tell that! Why did she come and take her?"

Jesse shook his head. "We don't know much yet. But you've gone the right way to let a lawyer handle it. We can approach the woman, sound her out about a possible adoption—see which way the cat jumps. Even barring anything else, it is just possible that if we got it before a judge, he'd let Josie make up her own mind."

"Oh, of course she'd say she wants to stay with us! But could we do that?"

Jesse didn't think it was very likely. He felt an immense sorrow for these good people, thinking of David Andrew at home. Even keeping them awake at night, but eventually to become a reasonable human being, and they'd brought it on themselves. As, of course, had the Lannings; but it was a human habit.

Lanning stood up heavily. "Well, you've got everything here—what addresses we know and so on. You'll be in touch with us, let us know what you think?"

"I'll be in touch. The first thing is to contact her and see what her attitude is." They nodded mutely at him and went out quietly, Lanning's arm around his wife's bowed shoulders. Jesse looked after them sadly; he could almost foresee the end of this one, and there wasn't much he could do about it.

Try to do what he could.

He wondered suddenly what the old man would have said about it . . . DeWitt and the always-very-much-suspect automatic writing. . . . Suddenly he grinned, hearing the old man say testily, *Tosh! Jesse, you got better sense than to swallow that.*

"Mr. Blythe's here," said Jimmy Gordon from the door.

"O.K.," said Jesse, snapping back to attention. The Acme damage suit, and that one questionable witness. He sat down and lit a cigarette.

When he slid the car into the garage at six-ten and came in the back door, Nell had everything under control. The baby was sound asleep in the hand-carved cradle old Mr. Walters had brought back from his visit to Hawaii; a casserole was in the oven, a salad in the refrigerator and Mrs. Frances Falkenstein Clock and Nell were cozily sipping Chablis and feeding Athelstane cheese crackers.

"Busy day, darling?" asked Nell.

"Confusing," said Jesse. "I could tell you a sad story." But he didn't immediately; he wandered into the dining room to build himself a drink, and almost at once went back for another as Sergeant Andrew Clock arrived. "You look beat, Andrew. Shall I make it a double?"

"You do that," said Clock dourly, going to kiss his bride. Athelstane rose up at him lovingly. "Sorry I'm late—thanks, Jesse." He accepted the Bourbon and water gratefully. "I swear to God, unidentified bodies! Another one just turned up, in an alley off Sunset, just at the end of shift." He had recently been transferred from the Robbery-Homicide office downtown to the Wilcox Street precinct, and was still getting used to the new beat, where the detectives handled any kind of case that turned up.

"I'd rather hear Jesse's sad story," said Fran, "if it's before dinner."

"Short and sweet," said Jesse, and gave it to them.

"But that's a tragedy!" said Nell. "Those poor people—nice people. Can you do anything about it, Jesse?"

"Remains to be seen," said Jesse, finishing his drink. "The phone company wouldn't oblige a mere lawyer—you might use your rank to get an address attached to this," and he passed over a scribbled phone number. It was the only thing he'd yet looked at out of the manila envelope.

TWO

On Saturday morning, with no office hours to keep, Jesse spread the contents of the envelope out on the coffee table and examined them over a third cup of coffee. There wasn't much of it, but this and that of interest, not only from the viewpoint of locating Nonie. The address attached to the phone number was Cahuenga Boulevard.

"Flibbertigibbet," he said to Nell some time later as she came in rattling her keys.

"What? I'm going out to the market, if you'll be here for the next hour." The baby had let them sleep last night, and she looked her usual trim self, brown hair in its accustomed fat chignon, shoulders and legs bare in a navy sun dress. "It's going up to ninety-five today, the radio said. And thank God for air conditioning and why we have to live in this climate—who's a flibbertigibbet?"

"Nonie," said Jesse. "I'll be here, but I've got things to do when you get back. You might take a look at this sometime and see how it strikes you." As she started for the garage, he was looking at the exhibits again.

Lanning had been thorough, keeping everything they'd had from Nonie; it wasn't much. There were four brief notes, four envelopes that had been through the mail, the slip with the phone number, two pictures. The first one was a snapshot in color: it was identified on the back in a square masculine hand as *Nonie and Josie*, a date six and a half years old. It was a candid shot of a slender blond girl holding a baby about two and a half. The baby was just a baby, dark hair and solemn eyes, but the blond was—Jesse decided the only word was "cute." She was barely dressed in a halter-necked skimpy sun dress; she had a triangular kitten face, young, innocent, appealing, a wide smooth brow, big eyes, a tiny chin. And a very nice figure. The other picture was a black and white portrait, head and

shoulders, not a salon job but the kind produced by school-class pho-
tographers commemorating graduations. Jesse looked at it with interest; it was labeled *Josie, graduation third grade.* Josie at eight didn't
look anything like her mother. She had very dark hair cut short in
something like a Dutch bob, and it was curly; she had big dark eyes,
a rather wide mouth, a serious expression. She looked like a nice little girl, and a bright one.

The notes said more about Nonie than the picture. All on cheap
dime-store tablet paper, carelessly folded, the hasty ballpoint scrawl
barely literate. *Sorry leav babby with you this long mabe this help.
Hope baby OK. Am out of work stayin hear with mom awile hope
babby OK. Hope this help som for kid.* Each note had been left in
its accompanying envelope. The first one was legibly postmarked *Las
Vegas;* the other postmarks were unreadable. On the third envelope
was a cheap return-address label pasted on: Mrs. Mabel Brock, an
address on 231st Place in Torrance. On the back of each envelope
the square masculine hand had noted tersely a sum of money origi-
nally enclosed.

Scatterbrain, said Jesse to himself. Not much education, however
long she'd attended school. The girl out for the fun times, with the
short attention span and not able or willing to think far ahead? Not
one to take to washing diapers and arranging balanced meals for
baby, by what the Lannings said. But a small conscience of a sort:
she had sent some money, however little. She hadn't quite forgotten
the baby.

And these notes went up to three years back. It was possible that
Nonie had matured a little. Maybe even was planning to get married
again? and was there, had there ever been, a legitimate father in the
picture? So much older and harder, said Sue Lanning: where had
Nonie been, what doing, these six years?

Nell came back about ten o'clock and said it was hell outside and
she was hibernating in air conditioning the rest of the day. Jesse said
absently he'd leave her to it. "I'm going to see if I can locate Nonie."

"That poor child—I hope to goodness you can do something
there, Jesse."

It *was* hell outside: still and humid and very muggy, and why such
hordes of people had settled in this climate was a mystery. Of course,

the settling hordes had contributed to the changes in climate with
the miles of cement and tall buildings.

The address on Cahuenga Boulevard turned out to be one of the
jerry-built-looking new garden apartments, about forty units in three
stories built around a center pool. Somewhere around two-fifty for a
one-bedroom, he could guess. A row of mailboxes in the lobby, two
of the little name slots empty, but no Johnson, no Brock. What had
she been calling herself? There was a manageress on the premises,
and he found her at home, a brisk and efficient white-haired woman,
Mrs. Fallon.

"Mrs. Johnson? Yes, she had Four-B, but she's moved. Yes, that's
her, young and blond—she looks younger in that picture"—as she
peered at the snapshot—"but that's her."

"Did she leave a new address?" Jesse passed over one of his cards.
"It's rather urgent that I talk to her."

"Oh," she said. "A lawyer." She looked at him curiously. "No, she
didn't. As a matter of fact she never let me know she was moving.
I've got no idea where. These young people—careless, they come and
go. Yes, that's the phone number in that apartment. I didn't really
think much about it, her going like that. She was working nights for
one thing, and it could be she tried to let me know and I just wasn't
in during the day. She could've left a note, but like I say, these
young people—careless. They just don't think. She wouldn't have
had much to move, her clothes, a few dishes maybe, they're
furnished units. She had a phonograph because the people in Four-A
were always complaining about it. What d'you want to see her
about?"

"A legal matter," said Jesse. "When did she move?"

"Well, it'd be about two weeks, ten days ago. The rent was paid
to the end of this month, I hadn't any reason to go looking for her,
and I don't pay attention to when tenants come and go—one thing I
can tell you, she didn't have a car, how she got around I don't know,
buses or boy friends taking her, I don't know. Mrs. Miller in Three-B
had a leaky faucet, and when my husband went to fix it, she told
him she thought Mrs. Johnson had gone, no lights and the front
door open, and did she owe any rent. So we looked, and she had
gone. Closets empty, nothing personal around and stuff spoiling in

the refrigerator—these girls. That was about ten days ago, last week."

Funny, thought Jesse. Yes? Nonie coming to take Josie back, there'd been some change in her life-style, hadn't there? Why shouldn't it include a move? And according to what he could guess about Nonie, it would be quite in character that she'd absent-mindedly given the Lannings the old phone number.

"How long had she lived here?"

"I'd have to look it up—about a year. The rent was always on time, and aside from the phonograph she wasn't a bad tenant. Oh, parties sometimes, I guess she had boy friends hanging around, but that's young people." She shrugged. "No, I never heard any names of people she knew. Well, I can tell you where she works, if she's still there—place called the Tropico Club out on Sunset, she gave it as a reference when she moved in."

Getting back in the Dodge, Jesse felt annoyed at Nonie. These casual irresponsible people—no telling where the girl had got to. With Josie. He stopped at the first pay phone and looked up the Tropico Club; it wasn't far out on Sunset and he drove out there, without much expectation that it would be open.

It wasn't. It would be open, by the sign on the door, from 6 P.M. to 2 A.M. It was an old building standing alone, recently painted a garish pink, with its own parking lot. It was plastered all over with signs, front and both sides—TOPLESS! NUDIES! 3 FLOOR SHOWS NIGHTLY —NUDES—TOPLESS BOTTOMLESS CUTIES!

The traffic was slower than usual, the streets looked dirtier in the building humidity past the down-at-heel old sections of the city: Huntington Park, Inglewood, Hawthorne, down to Torrance twenty miles from Hollywood. The address on 231st Place was a single house on a narrow lot, crowded against its neighbors, an old frame house needing paint but with a strip of green lawn in front, flower beds at the sides. Jesse parked in front and on the tiny porch pushed the bell beside the front door; that was open behind an old screen door. A woman appeared and looked at him, wiping her hands on a dish towel.

"Mrs. Brock? I'm trying to find your daughter Mrs. Johnson." He proffered a card. She opened the screen a crack and took it.

"You a lawyer? What you want with Nonie, is she in some kind of trouble?"

"Not that I know of." She looked a very ordinary woman: dowdy in a cotton dress and apron, sandals on bare feet; she was thin and angular, looking older than she probably was, thin gray hair unwaved, a faintly sour expression. "I just want to talk to her. She's moved recently and didn't leave an address—would you know where she's living?"

She shook her head slowly. "I haven't seen Nonie in a year or so. Never lay eyes on her unless she's broke and comes to ask for something. We all got troubles, and I'm not one to complain, the Lord sends 'em to try us."

"I understand she was married—the baby's father—"

"A-course she was married. Nonie's done things I didn't approve of, but she was raised right like all my three girls, you got no call to say—" It wasn't fierce defense; she sounded merely tired. "I told her she was a fool to marry that kid, hardly older'n she was, just a bum —a no-good bum, hanging around with the same kind, guitars, long hair—bums. I wasn't surprised he walked out on her. What d'you want with Nonie, anyway?"

"Was there a divorce?" asked Jesse. Better try to get the legal picture clear.

"I dunno. Nonie never said about divorcing him."

"Well, does she see her sisters much? Would they be likely to know where she is?"

"You could ask Chris, I s'pose," she said reluctantly. "Martha wouldn't know—she's got no use for Nonie after we found out she was working in that place."

"The Tropico Club?"

Her mouth tightened. "I guess you know about that. No clothes. Chris might know about Nonie—my other girl. She lives in Hollywood. Her name's Lefkowitz, she married another bum but she got shut of him. It's Manhattan Place."

"Well, thanks very much." Not, reflected Jesse, what might be called a close family. Evidently no Mr. Brock anywhere around; another no-good bum?

If Nonie was still working at the club, he could catch her there eventually. But now he was wondering about that.

He found Christine Lefkowitz listed in the book, Manhattan Place in Hollywood; it was one of the old brick apartment buildings dating from the twenties. She lived on the top floor, but there was no answer to the bell.

And so what now, he wondered. It looked as if he'd be doing a little more work for the Lannings than he'd figured.

He couldn't ask questions at the night club until six at least. He drove back to the office and spent an hour going over that contract, making notes for its amendment in his finicky copperplate, left those on Jean's desk and went home.

"It looks," he told Nell, "as if I visit a topless bar tonight. Could we have an early dinner?"

◎◎◎

It was smaller than it looked from outside, dark and redolent of stale liquor, past crowds. The double front doors let him into a small square lobby; there were shabby pink velvet curtains across a doorway six feet ahead. It was just past six, but there didn't seem to be anybody around. Jesse pushed through the curtains and found himself in the main body of the place, a room about a hundred feet square with little tables scattered around, a long bar at one side, a raised stage at the far end now draped with a sleazy-looking pink curtain. A paunchy white-aproned bartender was indolently busy behind the bar, another man perched on one of the stools. They both glanced around as Jessie came in.

"Early bird," said the second man genially. "Haven't seen you around before, welcome."

"I'm looking," said Jesse, "for Nonie Johnson. I understand she works here."

"Yep. Harry Mortensen, me," and the second man offered a pudgy hand. "I own this joint. Why you want Nonie?" He took the offered card and peered at it, holding it to one of the dim red lamps spotted on each table and along the bar. "Hey, lawyer, hah? Somebody leave Nonie a million?"

"Not that I know of. She does work here? Waitress, or one of the dancers?"

"I don't waste money on waitresses, let the guys wait on themselves," said Mortensen with a grin. "She's in the show. Or—well, I couldn't say exactly where she is right now, at that. She's a good kid, but these kids, they get restless, they come and go. What the hell, she wants to take off for a little vacation, it's O.K. by me, she can have the job back, she shows up. If she don't, easy to get another girl, but I expect she'll turn up. Nonie's worked for me a coupla years, she's a good kid. What the hell's a lawyer want with her?"

Jesse felt exasperated, meeting Mortensen's vacant, vacuous, friendly grin. Mortensen was in his fifties, fat, sharp-dressed in flashy sports clothes: the hail-fellow-well-met who obviously wasn't given to deep thought about anything.

"When did she take off?" Jesse asked.

"Hell, last week, ten days ago. Just didn't show, and I asked the other girls but they said she hadn't said nothing, but we think she went with Big Boy, see."

"Big Boy," said Jesse gently. "A boy friend?"

"Not her regular. This is one of the guys comes in, he's here a lot, and he sure goes for Nonie. Some guys like the ones—you know"— he gestured—"not so bazoomy, but Nonie's got a real good figure, proportioned like they say, you know? He's been hot for her, and she always turned him down before but hell, he was loaded and no chick in her right mind'd turn down a Caribbean cruise like he talked about."

"A cruise," said Jesse. "Money? What's his last name?"

"What the hell is it?" Mortensen asked himself. "I don't remember people's last names. Big Boy. He's a great big guy, about forty, sharp clothes, pair of shoulders like a football pro. He's a salesman some kind. What the hell's his name, Barney?" He appealed to the bartender, who just shook his head. "I'd sure as hell like to know what you want with Nonie," said Mortensen.

"Private business. I suppose the other girls might know? They here now? Could I see them?"

"Sure," said Mortensen. A few other customers had come in, drifted up to the bar. "Yeah, they'll be here—first show's at seven. You can come round to the dressing room. They're all good kids, I got a good thing going here, full every night, and I treat the girls right, no funny stuff from the customers allowed. If the girls want to play along with some guy theirselves, that's different, see, up to them. You got to admit that's the fair way to handle it, Mr. whatever the hell that card said." He was leading Jesse down one side of the room, past the stage, to a door under one stage apron. "Straight ahead. I oughta put in some bigger lights here, but what the hell." He knocked on a door to the left. "Hey, girls, you decent enough to see Harry? I got somebody wants to meet you." Without waiting for an answer he barged in, and Jesse followed him.

The three girls in the stuffy little room were all dressed, after a fashion, and didn't look perturbed at the invasion. One blond, two brunettes, and Nonie would fit in, Jesse thought: just by her picture, what he'd heard, the same type. Whatever the state of their morals, the girls out for the good times, and like Mortensen not thinking very much or very often about anything beyond that. "Hey, girls, what you know, this is a lawyer looking for Nonie. I told him about that Big Boy guy—any of you remember his last name? And what the hell's your name again?—oh, yeah—this is Barbie, Lily, Linda."

"I don't think Nonie went off with him," said the blond indicated as Barbie. "He's kind of a drag—like a big kid. Sure, he's got the bread but that isn't everything."

"But she said he was talking about an ocean cruise," said Lily. "On a real big ship, like. It sounded neat— Yeah, his last name's Pierce."

"She didn't mention anything definite to you?" asked Jesse. "As to where she was going, when? She didn't quit her job here?"

"Naw," said Mortensen. "She never said a thing to me, just took off. But say something came up all of a sudden, this guy called and said let's go, that's probably what happened."

"She wouldn't, with him," insisted Barbie. Linda was absorbed in applying lipstick, bent close to the stained mirror. "Nonie's got a regular boy friend already, that guy always meets her after the last show. His name's McAllister," she informed Jesse. "Rog. He's jealous as hell of her, he don't like her working here except the money's good."

"Are they living together?" asked Jesse.

She shrugged. "Who cares? All I know about him is his name and what she said. He's good-looking. Kind of an Orlando type, real dark and tall."

Linda recapped her lipstick and deigned to look at Jesse for the first time. "What's a lawyer want with Nonie? She in some trouble?"

"Not yet," said Jesse.

"Oh. Well, I figure like Harry says, she's off with that Big Boy. Because I can tell you something about this Roger. He hadn't been the boy friend, steady, for all so long—maybe six, seven months. And that night—you know, Lily—when he called and said he couldn't take her home, his car on the fritz, so I drove her home—"

"To the apartment on Cahuenga?" asked Jesse.

"Yeah, that's right. She was talking on the way. About how she was really off Rog, he was always after her, do this, do that, try to run her whole life. She wasn't so crazy about him at all. She said he was ready enough to borrow money even if he didn't like her earning it dancing here. If you ask me, she went off on that cruise with Big Boy, and I just hope she's having a good time. Because it was about the same time, see."

"The same time what?" said Mortensen. "Oh, yeah, I get it, sure. He's in usually four, five nights a week, but he hasn't been, last couple of weeks. So he's probably on that Caribbean cruise. And it was right about then Nonie didn't show."

"Does anybody know where Pierce works?" asked Jesse resignedly. It could be that Linda and Harry had the answer, or did they? What about Josie?

"He's a car salesman," said Lily. "I think he works for some relative, he said something once, an uncle or father or something, I didn't pay much attention. He's not so bad, Barbie, just like a big kid, and real generous, when he heard about my birthday last month he gave me ten bucks. He's really a nice guy."

"Did she ever say anything to any of you," asked Jesse abruptly, "about her daughter?"

They looked at him. "Nonie? Did she have a kid? We never heard about that," said Barbie.

Jesse stared at his half-smoked cigarette, and a new little story dovetailed in his mind. It pieced together, in a way. The simple nice guy Big Boy, with money; the fun-loving simple girl Nonie, fed up with the recent boy friend. It could be that those two had slipped over to Vegas and got married. Change in life-style that would be, all right. And something coming up about the other marriage, the baby, the nice guy saying, you ought to have your own kid, take care of it right, now.

That presupposed a divorce.

But that had been at least ten days ago, or thereabouts, and Nonie had come to take Josie only last Sunday. Called to announce it a week ago tonight.

So it could be that Nonie and Big Boy had been on a few days' honeymoon, say in Vegas, and then decided to take Josie along on the cruise.

He dropped the cigarette and stepped on it. At least, this looked like a dead end. But if that was the way it had gone, they'd be back eventually. He hoped.

"Has she got any salary coming?" he asked Mortensen.

"Yeah, yeah, that's another reason I say she just took off awhile. I owe her for the first half of the month, three eighty-five. I said I do right by the girls."

At least car agencies were open on Sunday. If he felt like trying to chase down Big Boy. Working for a relative, who might be named Smith or Caruso or Epstein instead of Pierce.

"So, thanks very much," he said.

"I'd still like to know what you want with Nonie," said Mortensen wistfully. "You better stay for the show, it's real hot, you come on out front and I'll buy you a drink, Mr.—I never remember names—"

"No, thanks," said Jesse. He'd seen all of Barbie, Linda and Lily he wanted.

◎◎◎

Lorna Hudson regarded her employer interestedly. A lot of funny things happened in this business, and he was one of the best at handling funny things. "Shall I put in a call to Mr. Galluci, Mr. Quiller?"

"For Chrissakes, baby, fetch a lawyer in it and make the headlines? Are you nuts? No, I tell you, I want you to see this broad. Just quiet and nice, dear. Don't do any talking, just listen. And come and tell me what she's got. You can do that, baby—no sweat."

Lorna didn't bat an eye. She'd done funnier things in the course of the job. "Where and when?"

"She'll call back. Put her straight through and I'll set up a date.

Jesus, why I ever got into this rat race—but it'll be no bread out of my pocket. If I could just get hold of Vic, damn it—and don't tell me I'll get hell with the lid off from him, the goddamn miser—but hell, we don't know it's not a bluff. Just a tale. You go and find out, baby."

"Anything you say, Mr. Quiller," said Lorna demurely.

It seemed to Josie it'd been years since she left home.

It was seven days, eight days today. It felt like eight hundred, and then it didn't. Home was just a little way off, really, only eight days ago.

But the days had changed, everything was different.

She didn't even know where she was, because she'd been so scared she couldn't notice which way the car went or how long it took to get here. Wherever here was. Still Los Angeles, but that was a big place.

She hadn't been that scared because of the strange lady they said was her real mama, or what Mother Sue tried to tell her about it. She'd been scared, but not like *that* till just at the last—the look in their eyes, Daddy Fred's, Mother Sue's, and they hadn't done anything. To stop Mama taking her. So fast, right at the last, Daddy Fred really shouting and Mama pulling her out the front door and Mother Sue crying, Josie had never seen her cry before and it did something awful to her insides, and her suitcase—

What with them trying to explain, that night, that morning, and things happening so fast, not an awful lot was in the suitcase. Not enough. Two school dresses and six pairs of panties and six pairs of socks, she'd had on her Sunday-school dress but it was all wrinkled and dirty now. Her hairbrush and a comb and toothbrush, and only four books.

There hadn't been anything to do all week. Mama was gone a lot. Josie had tried to remember her—her real mama, they said—but she just couldn't. Ruthie Graham in her class at school was adopted, there wasn't anything wrong about being adopted, but Mother Sue talking about a court of some—

She hadn't any more clean underclothes.

Right here, all the eight days. She hated this place with a dreary sort of hatred, all four cramped, dirty, horrible rooms. It was an apartment where Mama lived, and the man named Denny. Everything was old and dirty. They'd told her the little bedroom was hers. It had an old saggy couch to sleep on, and not much else in it, a chest with three drawers but they were full of clothes already. There was just an old window blind at the window and it didn't wind up or down. Across the street was a big neon sign that went on and off: EATS EATS EATS. You could feel it there even when you shut your eyes.

The man was there mostly. He was sort of nice, like trying to be friendly, calling her "honey" and "cutie."

Last night, the macroni and cheese, and bread with a cheesy spread. "I'm not supposed to eat cheese," she said politely, and Mama was mad.

"Eat it or go hungry, baby."

Denny had tried to be nice. *Don't be like that, kitten, the kid don't like it, I go and get her a hamburger.* But he hadn't.

There wasn't anything to do here. When she asked, he said you don't want to go outside, too hot, no place to play. He just sat around mostly, smoking cigarettes and looking at magazines.

Josie sat on the old couch and looked at her four books. *The Wind in the Willows. A Child's Garden of Verses. The Jungle Book. Dr. Doolittle's Circus.* She knew all of them nearly by heart except the *Jungle Book,* she'd just got that one for her graduation from fourth grade, and it had been exciting to start, but right now she just didn't feel like reading anything.

And where'd she go to school when the new term started next month? Nobody said.

It was getting dark outside and the neon sign started to flash on and off. EATS.

She heard the apartment door open. Mama coming back. She was talking to Denny. He called her funny names; "kitten," "kit-cat," "spit-cat." He was nicer than Mama. But Josie couldn't tell Denny about not having any clean underclothes.

Getting dark, on Sunday. At home, Mother Sue would be getting dinner, and Daddy Fred smoking his pipe and reading in the living room, and Bix would be under Mother Sue's feet begging—

All of a sudden Josie could see and feel Bix, the cold wet nose and soft floppy ears and loving brown eyes, and without warning a great gulping sob shook her and she turned over on the couch and buried her face in the musty pillow.

◎◎◎

After the last show on Sunday night, Barbie Palmer's latest date met her and they went to a bash at Ken and Lisa's place. There were a lot of people drifting in and out, and some pal of Ken's peddling the speed if you wanted it but Barbie didn't go for that bit, the *vino* was just fine for any kicks she wanted.

Lisa used to work at the Tropico and knew Nonie, and Barbie told her about that lawyer coming, Nonie maybe on the cruise with a new guy. And what the lawyer said about her having a kid.

"I guess that could happen to anybody, no?" said Lisa. She giggled; she'd had a couple of joints already and was feeling happy. "She ditched Rog? Or maybe he ditched her. Last time I saw Nonie, she was stoned but good—that beach party last week or whenever—Rog had to carry her out to his car."

"I never saw her get that high."

"She sure was that night. Rog was mad as hell."

Then somebody turned on a phonograph and they started to dance. It got a little wild, and pretty soon the cops came knocking—neighbors complaining or something—and Barbie and her date took off.

◎◎◎

"That's really very satisfactory," said Elizabeth Duffy in her beautiful contralto voice. Her voice was the only beautiful thing about Miss Duffy, who was a plain girl, but extremely efficient. She slapped the pages of the carbon together and enclosed them in a manila folder. "It's interesting how the evidence dovetails, from all three sources."

DeWitt agreed absently, glancing over the pages of the top copy. What was interesting, he thought, was that it was the same kind of evidence showing up, the same sort of thing that filled all those records of the old organizations. This was the transcript of a very nice body of evidence indeed, coming through to one of their perennial sitters, Claire Ewing; like most of their sitters, a researcher herself, not an emotion-harried sentimentalist hunting reassurance. A piece of research all tightly tied up with the safeguards against the old, old argument over telepathy. Miss Duffy acting as proxy sitter; Mrs. Ewing never present at a sitting with any of three mediums. And the communications had come through, from the deceased husband: the pet names, incidents know only to the wife, the obscure references recognized. And the little bonus evidence, nothing new but interesting. The niece.

"We don't really know a thing about it, even after all this time, do we?" said Miss Duffy soberly. "The how and why, the—the mechanics. They seem to know a little more than we do, on this plane —to see a little way ahead, somehow. But not all of them. We just don't know."

"The old question of time and space," said DeWitt. "Not the same relationships of time or space in three dimensions—*here* equivalent to *now*—and then again, we're dealing with individuals, some better than others in the moral sense as well as others, some shrewder, some more concerned for us perhaps—" Not new evidence, but interesting. The husband's communication definitely predicting the imminent death of the niece, in four sessions with two mediums, up to two weeks ago; and yesterday afternoon the niece had died instantly in an accident, her car rammed by a drunk driver.

Telepathy, thought DeWitt with satisfaction, really didn't enter into this kind of thing.

"I wish," said Miss Duffy unexpectedly, "you'd show this to Mr. Falkenstein. Even he'd have to see there's something to it. I always feel he's—the doubting Thomas. The way he just never says anything."

DeWitt grinned at the transcript. "Oh, we don't have to convert Jesse—he's read all the solid evidence. It's just that, as the hardheaded lawyer, he likes the evidence to be airtight. I wish—" And he shut his teeth on the rest of the thought: that we could get the evidential communication through to Jesse. The old, old argument: telepathy between living minds explaining it all. That experienced researcher Doyle had once said that he considered telepathy to be much rarer than was supposed, and DeWitt was inclined to agree. But to exclude the possibility was imperative, just in case; and so, the proxy sitters. And no one here, Miss Duffy or the psychics, was aware that Jesse might welcome a communication. If anything ever did come through—

"There are," said Miss Duffy, "about two hours of tapes to check."

DeWitt said, "I'll take care of it."

"Thank you," said Miss Duffy in a subdued voice.

Miss Duffy, he was aware, was scared to death of the tapes. In a way, he couldn't blame her: that was, as Jesse said, but far out. But the most exciting breakthrough that had occurred in all the annals of research.

And didn't it make sense—didn't it, postulating the presence of all those individuals on the other side, many or most of them anxious to communicate—that after dealing with the imperfect human instruments of even gifted psychics, they should—perhaps with the guidance of mechanical experts—be interested in trying the purely mechanical means?

It could be a big breakthrough, and a very new one just in the last few years. Not much had really been done, no very solid evidence had turned up. But the possibility seemed to be definite from what had turned up. Pragmatic first principles established. Leave the tape recorder open, mike on, in the empty silent room; and sometimes, when you checked back with the volume up, there were the voices. The attempted communication between the entities there and here?

The tapes frightened Miss Duffy; in a sense they frightened DeWitt, but they excited him too.

⊚⊚⊚

When Fran called Clock at five-thirty he snarled at her. It was one of the days when he'd been wondering why he'd picked this thankless job. The old precinct house on Wilcox Street was a far cry from the modern, air-conditioned, efficiently equipped headquarters building downtown. He was only thankful that two of his best men, detectives Pete Petrovsky and Johnny Mantella, had been transferred along with him. With the crime rate up in central Hollywood as everywhere else, they now had seven heist jobs, four homicides, eighteen burglaries, one rape, two child molestations and the usual misdemeanors—shoplifting, petty theft, vandalism of schools—to do the paper work on.

"What do you want?" snarled Clock.

"So very loverlike," said Fran, amused. In the shabby workaday office Clock suddenly grinned, clearly seeing her, his lovely Fran—and family resemblances were queer, she and Jesse not really alike and yet an uncanny similarity in tone and laugh. "I just thought, in this heat wave, I really don't feel much like slaving over a hot stove."

"The air conditioning would run at least forty-five hundred," said Clock. They had recently bought the house on Hillcrest Drive, conveniently near Jesse and Nell if they should, in the future, need the free baby-sitters. The house wasn't air conditioned.

"Worth it," said Fran succinctly. "As long as we're going into debt anyway."

"I said we'd think about it."

"And Sally's off her food. No wonder, this weather."

"You didn't take her out in this heat?" Sally was their venerated black Peke, an unexpected legacy from Jesse's murdered secretary last January.

"Of course not. It'd be nice to be taken out to dinner. When you get home. Say Chasen's. With a long iced drink first."

"More money," grumbled Clock. "It's a deal. Call it forty-five minutes—I've got an autopsy report to read."

THREE

On Monday morning Jesse had to be in court to file a rather complicated will for probate, later for the Gulbrandsen divorce hearing. He
stopped by the office briefly; Jean said the amended contract would
be ready by noon. Jesse gave her Mrs. Brock's phone number. "You
might try to reach her, ask where this Christine Lefkowitz works, I
can't reach her at home."

He was in court until eleven-fifty, Mrs. Gulbranden's witness
delayed in traffic and the judge sarcastic. With the *decree nisi*
granted, he escaped from a grateful client and called his office. "Anything urgent come in?"

"Mrs. Gorman called, she wants to make a new will. Mr. Dakin'll
be in at three to see the contract," said Jean. "And I talked to Mrs.
Brock. She says Mrs. Lefkowitz works at the coffee shop at the Ambassador Hotel."

"Well, right close to home," said Jesse. "Thanks. I'll be back after
lunch."

The Ambassador wasn't the ultra-class place it had once been
years ago, but still a very good hotel: quiet class. He left the Dodge
in the parking lot and wandered past the shops in the lobby to the
coffee shop at one side of the block-square building complex. The
tables were sparsely occupied at this hour, the late-breakfast crowd
gone, lunchers not yet in. At an alcove to one side, where double
swing doors led presumably to the kitchen, a couple of bus boys and
three uniformed waitresses congregated: a fourth waitress was taking
an order from the couple near the alcove.

Interestingly enough, Jesse thought he could spot Christine Lefkowitz immediately, from the resemblance to Nonie's picture. He saun-
tered up to the little group and asked for her, and the one he'd
picked said, "That's me. So what can I do for you?"

"Like to ask you a couple of questions about your sister. Nonie Johnson." Jesse handed her a card. She looked at it and at him, wary, suspicious, ready to be hostile.

"Look, I'm supposed to be at work. What's this all about? A lawyer? What's a lawyer want with Nonie?"

"You get a lunch break, I suppose. Just a few questions. I'm trying to locate her."

"Oh," she said. She lowered her gaze to the card and after a moment said, "I'm not off for lunch till one, but I can take a break, we're not busy."

"Suppose we sit down someplace and have some coffee.

"We're not supposed to sit in here—" She looked at the nearly empty room, shrugged. "I guess Henry wouldn't mind. I'll get some." Jesse slid into a booth against the wall, and she brought two mugs of steaming black coffee, slid onto the opposite bench. "So what's this about? Is Nonie in some kind of trouble?"

"Just because I'm a lawyer?" Jesse regarded her with interest. He'd picked her out of the little group instantly, just on the strong resemblance to that candid shot of Nonie: but there'd be more to her than there was in Nonie, he thought. She had the same triangular face, high cheekbones and narrow jaw, taffy-blond hair unbecomingly gathered in a snoodlike net, but there were regulations about that for waitresses, likely when she was off duty she'd leave it loose. She looked about thirty, she had a taut trim figure in the yellow and white cotton uniform and her pale blue eyes were watchful on him. "Could you tell me where Mrs. Johnson's moved?"

She took her time. "Why you looking for her?"

"No trouble, unless she wants to make it," said Jesse, adding cream to his coffee. "It's like this." He explained economically about the Lannings, about Josie, and she listened without comment. "You can see their position. They've had the child nearly all her life, and when Mrs. Johnson suddenly showed up and wanted her back, it was a shock. They just want the chance to put their case to her, maybe come to some arrangement. For a start, I want to find her—find out what prompted her to want Josie back, for one thing. Did you know anything about this?"

Christine Lefkowitz sipped black coffee without raising her eyes, set the cup down, brought out a cigarette. Jesse offered his lighter.

"Thanks." She emitted a long stream of smoke. "No," she said after a pause, "no, not a thing. Are these people going to make a stink about it? Go in court or whatever?"

"They're not in any position to do that. Mrs. Johnson's the legal parent, the Lannings haven't any possible claim to the child legally speaking. But humanly speaking—Josie'd hardly remember her own mother, the Lannings are the only parents she's ever known and it seems a little peculiar that after all this time Mrs. Johnson should suddenly decide she wants her."

"I guess so." Christine absently moved the silverware back and forth, making a little pattern around her coffee cup. "But they can't do anything about it, I see. I told Nonie she ought to put the kid up for adoption, when Joe walked out on her. That was before the kid was born. But she was just a kid herself—seventeen—and Mom and Martha worked on her, the Lord's will and crosses sent for us to bear, and she didn't." She was silent, and Jesse waited. "I guess," she said after a minute, "some women like kids, taking care of them and the housework and so on, and some don't. It could be if things had been different at home—but our dad got killed in a construction accident when Nonie was only three, I was seven—and the damn company weaseled out of paying a dime, said he was only temporary help and it was his fault or something, Mom didn't get anything. She always had to go out to work, we all did soon as we could, anything we could get. None of us bothered finish high, Mom used to keep at me, go learn typing, shorthand, get a better job—I'd hate an office like poison, and it's not that much better pay. Mom and Martha talking about the Lord's will," and her mouth drew tighter. "You're going to get anywhere, I figure you got to forget about the Lord's will." All that was half to herself; she looked at Jesse and squashed her cigarette in the glass ashtray. "You want Nonie's address?"

"She's moved from Cahuenga Boulevard. Do you know where? Seen her lately?"

"Gee, I'd have to think when. A week ago last Tuesday. My day off. She didn't say anything about moving, or all this. She was just the same as usual." Her eyes were still wary.

"She mention anything about a fellow named Pierce?"

"No, why?"

Jesse told her about Big Boy. "Girls at the club seem to think she could have taken off with him. But if so, why'd she suddenly want Josie back? Can you tell me anything about her current boy friends, singular or plural? She'd never got a divorce from Joe? Any idea of getting married again?"

Christine laughed. "Nonie might not have much sense but she's got more than that, mister—take another chance, after that first bastard she got stuck with? Same like me—maybe the millionaire comes along, fine, but that'll be a cold day in hell one shows up here, or that third-rate night spot. Nonie never had the money, pay a lawyer for a divorce, and what was the point anyway? Sure, she had the boy friends off and on ever since, nothing serious."

"The latest one this McAllister. What about him?"

"He's just a guy," said Christine. "It wasn't anything serious, he's just somebody to go round with."

"He went to the Tropico, she met him there?"

"God, no. Men are damn funny," said Christine. "He isn't anywhere near a saint, who is, but he was always at her about the club, the topless bit. She never actually said so but I got the notion he was into her for some money, though. Men. No, he used to live in the same building on Cahuenga, shared with some other guys, that's where she met him. She never said anything to me about this Pierce." After another silence she glanced at Jesse and away, lighting another cigarette before he could reach his lighter. "Listen," she said, "Nonie's kind of soft some ways. She'll take some notion in her head and forget it the next day."

"Impulsive," said Jesse.

"You can say it again. I couldn't say what she might be up to, but I guess you could tell those people—whyever she took the kid, I don't see her keeping it long. She'll get fed up, a kid's a nuisance have around. Tell you something, I never heard the straight of that anyway, I thought the kid was adopted out."

"Well, that's not much immediate help," said Jesse. "She does keep in touch with you, though? If you hear from her, I'd be obliged if you let me know."

"Sure, glad to. I'll tell you who else you might ask too. Nonie isn't all buddy-buddy with the other girls at that club, just casual. I guess about her closest girl friend is Rena Sawyer. She used to work there too, but she got married last year to this Jim Sawyer. I think they

live in Burbank. Maybe she'd know something. And I hear anything
from Nonie, I'll let you know. I guess those people would be kind of
worried about the kid, come to think."

"Thanks very much."

"No sweat." As he slid out of the booth she was lighting another
cigarette from the stub of her last one.

That was a little exercise in futility, he thought, except for the
faint light it cast on Nonie's home life: deducible background.

He went back to the office, told Jimmy to send out for a sandwich
and got Lanning on the phone at home. "Here we go round the mul-
berry bush. Whyever or whatever, the girl's just not around. But the
consensus seems to be that she'll be back anytime, and when we can
locate her—" He enlarged on that, and Lanning listened patiently.

"But, Mr. Falkenstein—if she's gone off with some man, as you
suspect, why on earth did she want Josie?" Lanning was abrupt and
bewildered. "It doesn't make any sense!"

"Not much, apparently."

"God knows, if the woman really thought anything of her, had
any maternal feeling—even after six years—we'd have been willing
to discuss it, give and take—but, damn it," said Lanning, who probably didn't say that very often, "damn it, it's—as if she'd boarded a
dog with us and just—"

"And not even paid the bill in full," said Jesse without humor.
"There's not much we can do until we locate the woman. But she's
due some salary, she'll be back sometime for that. I take it you don't
want to go to the expense of a private detective—that can run high."

"How much?"

"With expenses, three hundred a day."

"Oh, my God," said Lanning, sounding tired. "I haven't got that
kind of money, Mr. Falkenstein."

"No. It's six of one, half dozen of another anyway. A private eye
might not locate her, and as I say the chances are that she'll come
wandering back, tomorrow, next day, from wherever she's been. And
I've got a couple more people to see. I just thought I'd bring you up
to date."

"I don't know how to tell Susan about this. What you say about
this man she may be with—what sort of life she's been living, that
night club—to think of Josie subjected to— My God," said Lanning.

"And I can't help feeling it's my fault, that I didn't do something about it years ago, take some positive steps to get legal guardianship or—just supinely hoping nothing would happen, we'd never see the girl again, don't rock the boat. If I'd done something—"

"Not much you could have done," said Jesse. "Just hold the positive thoughts, Mr. Lanning. We may find her tomorrow."

"I don't know how to tell Susan," said Lanning, and now he sounded frightened.

Jimmy came in with a ham sandwich and the information that he had an appointment at one o'clock. Eating the sandwich, Jesse reflected on the handful of nothing that he'd dredged up about Nonie. It was not only nothing, it was less than nothing. The lightweight scatterbrain Nonie, the topless dancer, the girl whose small glimmer of conscience over Josie had apparently faded out three years ago—the only hint of any immediate future plans Nonie might have had was of the Caribbean cruise with Big Boy. What in hell had sparked off her conscience again—if it had been? Her latent (very damn latent) maternal feelings? Suddenly descending on the Lannings and wanting Josie back?

He got up and went out to the secretarie's office. "You might try to reach this Mrs. James Sawyer, said to live in Burbank," he said to Jean. "Said to be a close friend of Nonie Johnson. Mrs. Rena Sawyer. I'd like to see her."

"That awful thing, the child. What gets into people," said Jean. "Mrs. Gorman's due in at two."

"That'll be the seventh will she's made," said Jesse.

In the press of business the rest of the afternoon, he pushed Nonie and Josie to the back of his mind. The new client wanted a divorce, Mrs. Gorman took an hour to talk about the new will and the D.A.'s office called about the Acme damage suit; they were thinking of prosecuting, which would be a break for Jesse's client. It was ten minutes of five when he was free.

"I'm getting out of here before anybody else comes in," he told the Gordons. "There's no hurry about getting that will copied, I wouldn't put it past her to come up with some changes tomorrow."

But he didn't head for home at once; he drove out to Cahuenga Boulevard and that big new garden apartment.

"Mrs. Fallon the Efficient" could answer the question promptly.

"Several young men sharing an apartment? More than two? That'd be Mr. Jarvis and his friends in Fourteen-A, I could think. The apartment's in Mr. Jarvis's name but there are four of them—nice quiet tenants. I couldn't say if any of them's home now, they've all got jobs, of course, but I only know about Mr. Jarvis, he works at a theater somewhere."

Jesse wandered around the pool and down a second court looking at door numbers. If nobody was home, leave a card and ask Jarvis to call him; few people could resist an invitation to call a lawyer about some unspecified matter. But he found Ben Jarvis at home in Fourteen-A.

Jarvis was about thirty, sandy, friendly, incuriously grateful for someone to talk to. "God, this heat," he said, shutting the door on the blast of humidity outside. "I'm lucky, have an air-conditioned place, and to work in, too." It appeared he was a projectionist at a movie house in West Hollywood. "Offer you a drink? What can I do for a lawyer? I can't call to mind I've got any rich relatives—or black sheep ones either."

"Roger McAllister," said Jesse. "He used to live here?"

"Oh, Rog. Why, what's he been up to? Yeah, he did. See, these two-bedroom places here are three-fifty per, with the pool and all, the only way any of us could make it is to double up. Four of us. It started out with me, Bill Woodin, Dick Meeker and Rog, but then Dick got married, and Rog moved before that. Then Bob Wheeling came in and George. It works out fine because George and I both work nights, he's a security guard at Universal Studios, and you can see—"

"Why'd McAllister move? When?"

"Well, Rog—some people like more privacy than others, I guess," said Jarvis vaguely. "Rog never really fitted in anyway." He looked uncomfortable. "Hell, I don't like to put it this way, sound snobbish about it, but he didn't—well, have the same background as the rest of us—education and so on. Rog is a good guy, only kind of a loner. And then he wasn't making as much as the rest of us, I guess it was a little strain to pay his share. He was only here three, four months. It was about last February he went and George came in. Why, what do you want with Rog?"

"Have you seen him since? Know where he's living?"

"Well, I haven't. Actually it was Dick suggested him, none of the rest of us—the original crowd—knew him before. Sure, he was working at a bowling alley on Highland, that's where Dick got to know him. He's the day manager there, or was. The Rink, it's called. I don't know where he moved to. Why are you—"

Jesse thanked him, refused the renewed offer of a drink and drove home through the heavy humidity, the cloying smog. Air conditioning greeted him in the house on Rockledge Road in the hills above Hollywood. The monster Athelstane was alseep on Nell's feet in the living room, and Nell looked up from her book with a start.

"Heavens, is it that late? I haven't even thought about dinner—"

"Interesting book? I'm early," said Jesse, turning his head to squint at the title. Prince's *Noted Witnesses for Psychic Occurrences*. "Don't tell me I've convinced you to read some of the classic literature. Where'd you get that?—I don't own a copy."

"The library. Mr. DeWitt mentioned it. It's a scream," said Nell inelegantly. "The stately Victorian style. All 'whilsts' instead of 'while.' The suffragette leaders and notable politicians and eminent scientists. And I've fallen madly in love with the British army colonel."

"Which one is that?"

"The lovely stern silent one who didn't want to alarm his wife. He just wrote in his diary, *Saw a ghost*."

Jesse grinned. "That one. Afraid you're not appreciating the classic evidence."

"Oh, I am," said Nell. "I hope you don't expect dinner right away. Sit down and relax, have a drink, I'll put something frozen in the oven. Veal parmigiana or lasagna?"

"Veal." Jesse drifted into the bedroom, stripping off his tie, and wandered down to the nursery for a fond look at David Andrew, who was staring dreamily at the ceiling and favored his parent with a secretive smile before suddenly falling asleep. Jesse went out to the kitchen and got down the bottle of Bourbon. "You?"

"I'll have what's left of the Chablis. Dinner in forty minutes."

Jesse carried his drink back to the living room. "Speaking of Victoriana, I feel I'm developing a taste for low characters," he said, sliding down on the end of his spine in the big leather chair. "That Nonie girl. No, I haven't found her. Chris. That one's smarter, if no

better morally. Rog. Big Boy. The topless dancers. Only thing I'll say
—"

"But where on earth could she have gone?" said Nell. "Oh, I
know, that type—drifts. Hither and yon. But when she'd just taken
Josie—I can see the likeliest thing really is the cruise, a girl like that.
But where would Josie come in? It's either one thing or the other."

"Come again?"

"I mean, she's got to feeling guilty about Josie, or all of a sudden
feeling maternal, grown up enough to—to realize responsibility, and
taken her back, really meaning it, feeling remorseful, if that's the
word I want. Or she's just the same as she was six years ago and gone
off for a good time with Big Boy. You can't have it both ways."

"Q.E.D.," agreed Jesse. "It's funny. And I've somehow got a feeling that Chris female knows something she hasn't parted with. What
it might be, no idea. It could be, though, that Nonie runs to confide
in big sister, even ask advice. The only thing that does occur to me,
with just the bits and pieces we've got on Nonie, there's a prima
facie case for getting her declared an unfit mother. Depending on
the judge. Judges can be funny too. And then there is the fact—"

"Yes?" said Nell encouragingly as he stopped.

"Well, people come all sorts. Some who do a lot of thinking and
feeling inside don't talk much about it. Others— I was going to say,
it's remotely possible, the growing-up thing. That Nonie's been—um
—thinking and feeling about Josie, sorry about it and realizing her
responsibility—deciding to do something—and just never mentioning it to anybody. But what we've heard about Nonie, I don't think
she's that kind. Think whatever was on her mind'd come out to anybody she talked to. And even if she did talk about it to big sister,
why should big sister keep it a secret?"

"And Mrs. Lanning said she didn't want her back," said Nell.
"Not really. A woman would know a thing like that, Jesse."

"Probably. Yes, what Lanning said today—if Nonie had come,
said something like that, wanted to make amends, they'd have given
her the chance. Still feeling sorry. Good charitable Christian people,
Nell. Beware the wrath of same. But she just—swooped and
snatched. Riding roughshod. Why?"

"I just can't imagine."

"Well—still a couple of people to talk to. Couple of possible leads. She's got to show up somewhere eventually. This ordinary dumb blond—"

"The more I think about it," said Nell, "Nonie doesn't sound so awfully ordinary."

◎◎◎

The bowling alley called The Rink was on Highland just north of Wilshire. It was a big garishly neon-lighted place, air-conditioned, and full of the happy bowlers at the shank of the evening.

There was a morose-looking man in a tan jump suit selling tickets at a booth outside the long lanes. He peered at Jesse's card and asked what a lawyer wanted with Rog McAllister.

"Just to ask him some questions about somebody. He's the day manager here? Do you know where he lives?"

"Not any more he isn't. He left last week. Last Wednesday it was. Had a little ruction with Mr. Davenport, he owns the place."

"Oh. He got fired, or quit?"

"Well, it was funny." They were both having to raise their voices over the noise in here, the hollow cannonlike boom of rolling balls and strikes, the loud hoarse voices, even though the ticket seller's little desk was a distance away. The man in the jump suit shifted comfortably in his chair, laid down his *True Detective* magazine; Jesse felt he was a welcome diversion in monotonous routine. "I'd just come on, and I was surprised to see Rog still here. He goes off at five usual, it's quiet till after about seven and the kid in charge of renting out shoes can take care of anybody comes in before I do at six-thirty, see. But Rog was here. It was payday, the fifteenth, and he'd waited to see Mr. Davenport—Mr. Davenport always pays us himself, and he was late. And Rog told him he was quitting. He didn't say it nasty, or sore, or ask for a raise or nothing. But I guess maybe Mr. Davenport was feeling sore about something, maybe had a fight with his wife, and he snapped back at Rog, job not good enough for you, you want more money, something like that. And Rog, he's got a temper on him too, he said what Mr. Davenport could do with the lousy job, he was coming in for a lot of bread and he wouldn't need the goddamn job."

"Oh?" said Jesse. "Did he say from where?"

"Nope. Just, he wouldn't need no job, going to live it up awhile on the fancy bread. Then Mr. Davenport sort of threw the envelope at him—with his pay in it, see—and went out, and I said had some rich uncle left him a bundle or what, and Rog just laughed and said never no mind, the bread was coming. He was acting kind of excited and right on top of the world. It was funny."

"Did he say anything else?"

"Yep. Two things. I asked him again where he was getting enough dough to quit a job—he'd worked here steady nearly three years —and he laughed again and said he got a straight tip on a real dark horse. Which was all the funnier, because the races aren't on now. Rog's a horse player all right, gets out to the track every chance he gets, but they aren't running now. Not till the harness races at the fair next month, and Rog doesn't go for them."

"And what else?"

"Why, he said first thing he was goin' to do was get him a good car. He's got an old clunker of an orphan, a Study Silver Hawk on its last legs, always conking out on him. He said he had his eye on a real sharp Mercedes in the used lot down the street."

"I see," said Jesse. "That's the last time you saw him? Do you know where he lives?"

"I saw him the day after, havin' a beer in the bar next to that used lot. Didn't talk to him, just saw him. He's been living at the Borland Hotel up in the next block, don't know if he's still there."

"Funny" was a word, thought Jesse on his way out. Whatever this was about McAllister, was it anything to do with Nonie? Unlikely. Another consensus seemed to be that the Nonie-McAllister affair was about *kaput*, and had never been more than casual. And nobody he'd talked to so far had any kind of money.

He left the car where it was and walked up to the next block, to the Borland Hotel. The night was muggy, breathless, heavy with the smells of old city streets; there were few people around, a huddle of dispirited-looking souls waiting at the corner bus stop, a couple of giggling teen-agers looking at a lighted jeweler's window. The Borland Hotel was grimy tan brick, a narrow four stories high; it had been there a long time. Jesse went in to a small square entry hall with a scarred counter across one side. There was a rheumy-eyed ancient in an old-fashioned silk undershirt and tattered blue serge pants behind the counter, ensconced in an old Boston rocker and reading *The Police Gazette*.

"Looking for Mr. McAllister," said Jesse.

The old man didn't bother to look up. "He's one of the permanents. Top floor, number eighteen."

Jesse climbed rickety uncarpeted stairs past windows long ago painted shut and glimpses of silent narrow hallways. You could say, no remote smell of money in this business at all. On the top floor he found a door marked 18 in smeary white paint, and knocked, but got no response at all.

He plodded downstairs again and started back for the car in the next block, but at the corner of the hotel building he slowed. There was a small public parking lot there, next to the hotel, with only four or five cars in it now: businesses along here mostly closed at night, no theaters, one bar nearly two blocks away. One of the cars, parked by itself up at the end of the lot, was an old Studebaker Silver Hawk. McAllister's? You didn't see many of those around any more, most of them departed to wherever good cars went.

If it was McAllister's, evidently he hadn't got around to dickering for the Mercedes. But he wouldn't get anything for the Study; he could have just walked off and left it.

Jesse climbed into the Dodge and headed for home and air conditioning. There, he found the baby awake, yelling, and a resigned Nell walking the floor.

"It was inevitable, of course," she told him, "that we'd produce a night owl. Both of us night people by nature. I just hope he'll settle down by midnight so we can get some sleep."

◎◎◎

On Tuesday morning Jesse left ten minutes early and stopped at the Borland Hotel, but McAllister still wasn't there, or wasn't answering the door. The Study was still in the parking lot.

The Gordon girls rode up in the elevator with him. "I got hold of Mrs. Sawyer after you left yesterday," said Jimmy. "She doesn't sound very bright."

"Any friend of Nonie's," said Jesse.

"She said she'd be home this morning if you wanted to see her. It's Brighton Street in Burbank."

"Have I got anything else to do this morning?"

"Not much for you," said Jean. "Us is something else. Your first appointment's at eleven-thirty. Unless they've rescheduled that divorce hearing."

They hadn't. Jesse groaned and said he'd better go see the damned woman. He didn't enjoy the drive, not that long on the freeway; but the car wasn't air conditioned and the air blasting through the open windows seemed to be made up of all the stale, fetid, gassy smells accumulated in the city for the last fifty years. The great arcs of sprinklers were on along the freeway, wetting down the pretty landscaping Parks and Recreation had planted on the banks. Not ten times as much money as Parks and Recreation had to spend could keep the vast acreage of foothills wetted down; for at least two, possibly four, more months they would bake all day, dry and dusty in this rainless climate, and let one brush fire spark off, there could be a holocaust all around the city. Why anybody had settled in this God-forsaken place he sometimes wondered, let alone why one of the world's great cities should have grown up here.

Burbank was quiet, even hotter. The address, when he found it, was a single house, a pretty little green stucco and redwood house beyond a green front lawn. The door was opened by a very pretty redhead in a Hawaiian muumuu. She opened wide green eyes at him and welcomed him in breathlessly.

"You're the lawyer's office that called. My goodness, what's it about? I couldn't imagine, Jim says I imagine things but I really don't. He said if you want a witness to that accident he felt sorry for the jury but I told the policeman I couldn't be sure which car and he was nice as anything. Oh, sit down. What is it about?" She perched on a chair opposite, looking anxious.

Jesse felt more depressed. This small front room was all consciously Early American, Salem maple furniture, a lot of bric-a-brac on shelves and tables, hobnail glass, little figurines, little patchwork throw rugs all over the floor, primitive rural prints in primary colors and fussy frames on the walls. Thank God Nell liked plain old-fashioned oak. He told Rena Sawyer he was trying to contact Nonie; had she seen her recently?

"Nonie? Is that all you want? Oh. The other thing I thought was, maybe somebody was dead. I don't know who it'd be, I've only got a couple of cousins. What about Nonie?"

"She's moved, I'm trying to locate her," said Jesse patiently. "Never mind what about, it's a long story, sort of private. Have you seen her lately?"

"We just got back off vacation yesterday. We rented a camper and went to Yosemite for a week. But I saw Nonie, it was the day before we left, or—no, it was that day. A Saturday."

"Sunday, if you got back yesterday after a week."

"No, it was Saturday. A week ago last Saturday," she said positively. "I met her in Hollywood and we had lunch and went shopping. She didn't say anything about moving. Why do you want to find her? You could see her at the club, she's still working there."

"She seems to have gone somewhere. Did she say anything to you about a new boy friend—about a man named Pierce?" Rena shook her head. "Did you know, incidentally, that she has a daughter?"

The green eyes widened more. "The baby? Oh, sure. It's funny you should ask me that, we talked about it that day, Mr. Epstein—"

"Falkenstein."

"Oh, excuse me. It's funny, because I thought about that since. No, I don't know where she's gone, she didn't say anything that day about going anywhere, or moving, only I do remember she said about this Big Boy guy, once before, I guess she liked him all right but nothing serious. But that sort of came up that day when we were having lunch, Musso and Frank's it was because I wanted to go to The Broadway, they were having a sale. Nonie's a real nice girl, Mr. Uh, maybe you know I first met her when I worked for Harry at the club too, only after I met Jim he didn't like it and I got another job in a store till we got married. But I guess I knew Nonie maybe a couple of months before she told me about that, that boy she married and the baby, and I didn't think much about it then but I did since. I felt kind of funny about it, about Nonie I guess, how she just left the baby with some people, oh, she said she sent money and all, but it seemed funny. I got to thinking about it and I couldn't have done a thing like that, I know it was awful, him walking out on her and no money and a baby takes a lot of time, but when it was your own — But she was kind of young—only I, well, I didn't feel just like I had before about Nonie. She said they were nice people and she sent money, but I just didn't. It's funny you should bring it up—"

The dumb redhead with some moral instincts; and if Jim could put up with the rest of her (the outside very nice, at least) maybe he hadn't made such a bad bargain. "A week ago Saturday," said Jesse gently. "The subject came up? What did she say?"

A blooming bright blush flooded Rena Sawyer's pretty, vacuous face. "Well, you see," she said proudly, "*I'm* going to have a baby. In March. And I was sort of asking her, you know, how it'd been for her and—well, you know—and it came over me again, how funny to have a baby and not see it for so long, and I asked didn't she ever wonder, or want to, I should think she would, and she said yes she did, she'd thought about it too and she did. She hadn't really wanted the baby then, Joe—her husband—he was mad about it, and he left her before the baby came and she sort of blamed the baby for that, she was crazy about him. She hadn't even thought about names, and when the nurse told her it was a girl and what would she name it, she didn't care, if it was a boy she'd have named it Joe, and the nurse said what about Josephine so that was why she did. But she said just like I said she had been thinking just lately—"

"I see," said Jesse to stop the spate. "Did she say definitely she'd thought about going to see the child, or—"

"I don't remember if she did or not, we were talking about my baby, that's how the names came up because it's going to be either Jim or Jewel. But she didn't say anything about moving or going anywhere, but maybe something came up all of a sudden, a better job or something—she was always talking about going back to Las Vegas, and maybe—"

If he was going to make his eleven-thirty appointment he'd have to be ruthless at cutting her off. He got up and thanked her for her help; if she heard from Nonie, would she call his office, good-bye.

She walked out with him to the car. "Gee, it's hot, isn't it? Jim says we can't afford air conditioning yet. I just thought of something, her day off's Monday, the club's closed then, and she usually calls me, ask what I'm doing, only she knew we'd be in Yosemite so she wouldn't have. If she does, like you said, I'll tell her you want to see her, only you never said what about, somebody dead or what. At least I can tell Jim it wasn't that accident, I told the policeman I couldn't be really sure—"

"Thank you very much," said Jesse loudly, letting in the clutch.

It was ten-fifty when he came off the freeway on the Santa Monica exit. He went down Beverly to Highland, wondering absently if Nonie —the creature of impulse—had suddenly succumbed, under Rena's prenatal influence, to her latent maternal feelings. And if so, what she had done since.

He caught the light at Highland and Sixth, and as he waited glanced half a block up to the Borland Hotel in the middle of that block. He had a little time on hand; on impulse he turned into the parking lot, found an empty slot, groped for change and then discovered he didn't need it. The local merchants, hoping to encourage trade, had temporarily bagged the meters: yellow tarpaulins over the meter heads, labeled *Courtesy of your local businessmen.*

He plodded up the stairs to the fourth floor, but McAllister still wasn't answering his door.

"Hell," said Jesse mildly, and plodded down again.

The Study Silver Hawk was still parked in the end slot of the lot, three slots from the Dodge. Idly he took the few extra steps to look at it.

◎◎◎

Clock was up to his ears in the paper work, in the continuing cases to work. Four more burglaries reported overnight, three more heists, another body—probably an O.D.—unidentified as yet. Mrs. Moorhead was coming in with her daughter, aged six, to try to identify whoever had tried to entice the daughter into a car yesterday afternoon; that could tie up to the definite molestation cases, and they had a good description on one of those.

When the phone rang on his desk he was reading another autopsy report on that body found last Saturday in an alley off Sunset. Female approximately thirty-five, description thus and such, O.D. heroin between noon and midnight 17–18 August. "Hell!" said Clock at the phone, and snatched it up violently. "Clock!"

"I'm sorry to bother you, Andrew. Expect you're busy."

"Busy!" said Clock. "What the hell do you want, Jesse?"

"Cops. I've just found a body. Apologies, but there it is," said Jesse sadly.

FOUR

When the Pontiac turned into the lot Jesse was waiting, leaning on the Dodge, hands in pockets. Clock and Petrovsky got out and went over to him. "Now what in hell have you turned up for us?" asked Clock.

"Same like old Jeshu ben Shira says," said Jesse, *"idleness teacheth much evil.* Wasn't any reason I should have gone to look, but I did, and there he was. Over there in the Study. Not nice, Andrew." Jesse nodded at stocky, snub-nosed Petrovsky.

Clock went to look, Petrovsky after him. The windows in the Study were all down; three feet away Clock's nostrils wrinkled. "Not nice. It's been here awhile, though in this weather—why wasn't it found before?"

"Local merchants." Jesse gestured at the tarpaulins covering the meters. "No officious meter maids checking overparked cars. And it's next to the alley. Anybody passing close, a lot of smells along alleys down here, people mind their own business."

"Who is it, you have any idea, Mr. Falkenstein?" asked Petrovsky.

"I don't know, but it could be one Roger McAllister. That could be his car." Jesse filled them in on that briefly. "Having a cop for a brother-in-law I knew better than to touch anything."

"The lab truck and morgue wagon are on the way." Clock leaned on the Dodge and lit a cigarette, rubbing his craggy prognathous jaw. "Your dumb blond snatching her own kid. This was her current boy friend?—if that's who it is. That's a funny one all right. I'll listen to all that again slower when we've heard what the lab boys say."

Jesse had already called the office to cancel his eleven-thirty appointment. The lab truck swung in and a couple of men got out. At the evidence of police activity a small crowd began to collect, and

Clock called up a black-and-white with the uniformed men to keep the people back. Presently the lab men got the body out onto a tarpaulin; it had been sprawled face-down in the cramped back seat of the Study.

"Well, there you are," said Clock, squatting over it distastefully. "It'll take an autopsy to say anything definite, but at a guess he's been dead a couple of days at least. Hard to say how, all the discoloration, but it doesn't look as if he passed out of a coronary. What about it, Jesse, is it McAllister?"

"I never laid eyes on him. By one description, it could be." The dead man was young, dark, big; he was wearing gray slacks, a green plaid cotton shirt, two-tone gray shoes.

"The car's registered to McAllister, Sergeant," said one of the lab men. "Roger A., address along here, the Borland Hotel. Looks to me as if he'd taken some punishment—bloody nose, marks on his jaw, that's not cyanosis. Whatever killed him."

"As if we needed another homicide," said Clock sourly. "Does this tie up to your blond, Jesse?"

"I hope not," said Jesse seriously. "I don't see how, Andrew. But" —he scratched his long nose—"I've got a handful of nothing on that, I really can't say. Like to know yes or no definitely. Like to know what you get on this, what shows up. Can I tag along awhile?" The lab men were methodically emptying the dead man's pocket onto another tarp; he went to squat over that with Clock and Petrovsky.

A little bunch of keys, two obvious car keys, two Yales. A cheap, small address book. Used handkerchief. A half-empty pack of Camel cigarettes. A matchbox about two by three inches, full of the little wooden matches some people prefer to book matches. A disposable butane lighter. A dollar and four cents in change. A tooled-leather wallet, not new. Clock flicked that open and said, "Well, it's him all right." In the first plastic sleeve, a driver's license: Roger Allen McAllister, and the usual head-and-shoulders I.D. shot. He'd been good-looking in a dark somber way: thick black hair, cut fairly short, sideburns, a straight mouth, a solid jawline. The description said six feet, a hundred and eighty pounds, black and brown, twenty-nine; the license was valid until next December. There wasn't anything else in the plastic slots, no snapshots or credit cards. The inside pocket held a wad of bills adding up to a hundred and thirty-four dollars.

"So he wasn't robbed," said Clock. "O.K., you can take him in." He stood up. "See if anything shows in the car, what an autopsy says. Pete, for a start we'd better have a look in the hotel."

Petrovsky had picked up the matchbox. "Those disposable lighters are pretty reliable, Andrew, as a rule."

"So what?"

"Making assurance doubly sure like they say—" Petrovsky turned the box over. "I just wondered—and there you are." He tossed it over to Clock, who looked at it and laughed.

"One of those. You can tag along, Jesse, and give me all that rigmarole again. About his quitting his job—and what about this blond? You said something about a possible new boy friend. Could have been a fight over the blond?" He started up the street toward the hotel. The morgue wagon arrived; the lab men were getting ready to tow the Study in.

"I'd doubt that. I just don't know enough, but I wouldn't think so. What's the matter with that matchbox?"

"Nothing," said Clock, sounding amused. At the hotel, the same elderly attendant was on duty behind the counter, and blinked at Clock's badge.

"Mr. McAllister? You mean the one lives here— Dead? You said dead? Why, he's just a young fellow—how can he be— In the parking lot out there? You mean, like he was mugged or— Be goddamned. Hardly safe to go out on the street no more."

"When was the last time you saw him?" asked Clock.

"I don't pay attention, the regulars here coming and going, why should I? I ain't always here. We don't get so many one-nighters like we used to." He licked his lips thoughtfully. "He wasn't in much. Young fellow, out a lot, prob'ly a girl, places to go, well as his job. He worked at the bowling alley down the street."

"We know. He ever bring a girl here?"

The old man tried to look indignant. "He did not. Wouldn't have been allowed, this is respectable. Besides, why should he, no kind of place to bring a girl. And besides that he broke up with his latest girl friend. I just remembered he said that, about a couple of weeks ago.

Had a fight with her and never wanted to see that fool blond again, he said."

"Oh," said Petrovsky. "Did he usually stop and gossip with you like that, coming and going? Then he probably told you other things —where he was bound for, how he spent his time when he wasn't at work?"

The old man looked from him to Clock. "No, he never. Why'd a young guy like that waste time on an old guy like me? He was in and out, 's all. I don't recollect he'd ever said much before, except about the weather or such. And you got no call third-degree me, if he got himself mugged it wasn't in here."

"Next door," said Clock. "Would you know if he was friendly with any of the other tenants here?"

After a minute the old man said sulkily, "Dave Archer, he's got seventeen next door, I think they knew each other some."

"We'll want a statement from you. You'd better think harder about when you saw him last," said Clock.

On the top floor, one of the Yale keys on McAllister's ring opened the door marked 18. It was a typical single bachelor apartment of this vintage, this kind of building and neighborhood: a shabby minimum of furniture in a small square living room, a tiny bedroom with barely space for a sagging double bed, a chest of drawers, a cubbyhole of kitchen with an ancient refrigerator, an unsteady table, an old apartment-sized gas range, a dank untiled bathroom. There was a film of dust and dirt over everything, more than a few days' accumulation; the stove and toilet were evilly stained, the bed unmade.

"Bachelor," said Jesse, looking around. "Place to sleep, eat occasionally. He wasn't here much, or what they call house-proud."

Clock shoved his hands in his pockets and wandered around the bedroom silently, and bent over the chest of drawers. Petrovsky opened the door to a slit of closet and said, "He spent a little money on clothes." There were seven or eight pairs of slacks, two suits, a little array of sports jackets, and six pairs of shoes on the floor.

"And these," said Clock. He picked up a deck of cards from the chest. Petrovsky took it, head on one side, and riffled through it.

"Nice. At inflated prices, about fifty bucks."

"Would you two professionals like to elucidate?" said Jesse.

Clock laughed, produced the matchbox and held it out. "Nothing abstruse. It looks as if McAllister was a gambler. This is what's called a shiner, Jesse—if you'll look close, you'll see there's a strip of mirror pasted along one side. Laid out all innocent on the table, at just the right angle, it gives you a nice peek at the other fellow's hand. And this is a deck of readers—marked cards. This particular deck's what's called edge work—there's a slight bevel along the edge of the cards, just some of them, you can feel it. Highest up for an ace, little lower for king, and so on. There are regular business firms make all this stuff, you can buy it by mail."

"I'll be damned," said Jesse. "But I said I didn't know anything about him. The fellow at the bowling alley said he liked to play the ponies."

"I'll bet," said Clock. "We can turn the lab loose here, but I don't suppose there'll be anything. Off the top of my mind, he just had an argument with somebody and got clobbered. The only funny thing is his being in the car, but it needn't have happened there. He could even have driven himself home before concussion caught up to him. Pending an autopsy, I'd say no female had anything to do with it— he wasn't any lightweight. Let's see if Mr. Archer's at home." He marched out and knocked on the door down the hall marked 17.

The man who opened it was obviously suffering a slight hangover, and they wasted a little time getting through to him. He was about twenty-six, slight and weedy, weak-chinned, still in faded pajamas and an old bathrobe; his bachelor apartment looked a good deal cleaner and neater than McAllister's. When it penetrated his mind that these were cops, that McAllister was dead, he said, shuddering, "Gah. My God, the poor guy. Excuse me, I got to have some more aspirin." He swallowed four in a copious draught of water, shook his head again and said, "My God. Like you need a convoy to go out in the street. The poor bastard. Yeah, I knew him—just from living next door, not good. He seemed an all-right guy. When'd it happen?"

"We're not sure. When did you see him the last time?"

Archer thought. "You got to excuse me, I kind of went off the wagon last night. Don't usually, but an old pal of mine's getting hitched this afternoon and we pulled a stag party for him. God, it's eleven-fifty, I got to think about getting dressed. McAllister? I saw him last Friday night when he came in, I guess that was the last time. I was just getting in too."

"From your job?"

"I'm on vacation, I'm a checker at a Safeway up on Sixth. That poor guy. Makes you think about getting out of what they call the inner city."

"Did he have many people come to see him here?" asked Petrovsky.

"Never knew him to have anybody. He wasn't here much."

"No, I don't suppose he was," said Clock. "You ever meet any girl friend?"

"No, but I heard about one," said Archer unexpectedly. "Why? What's with all the personal questions? I thought you said he got mugged."

"We're not sure yet. What about the girl friend?"

"I guess he just had to talk to somebody, I was handy. It was about two weeks ago, only time he was ever in my place. The door was open, it gets like an oven in these places this weather, and when he came upstairs he came in and was sounding off about this damn chick. How he found she'd been two-timing him, he had a big fight with her and he'd be off dames a good long time, you know the routine."

Jesse sighed and Clock shrugged. "You hadn't seen him since last Friday. Did he look the same as usual then?"

"Sure. I said hi, it was hot, he said it sure as hell was, and that was that. It was about midnight." Archer was curious now, wanted to ask questions, but Clock cut him short.

"So they'd had a fight," said Jesse back in McAllister's apartment. "Nonie two-timing him. Oh, yes? With Pierce?"

"I don't think your blond comes into this," said Clock. "I'd like to talk to her just in case, but by all this they'd broken up before she took off. You said that was last week? Whatever that rigmarole's all about, she didn't account for McAllister."

" 'Rigmarole' is a word," said Jesse. "But it's peculiar he should get himself killed just when—but it wasn't, of course, if they'd broken up."

"A lot of people get themselves killed for little or no reason these days," said Clock, stating a fact of life. "With the courts handing

out the reduced sentences, no death penalty. And"—he ran his handkerchief around his collar: this cramped stuffy place at the top of the
old building was probably ten degrees hotter than the street outside
—"extenuating circumstances sometimes. Tempers get set off. The
murder rate always goes up in a heat wave."

"I've got to get back to the office, damn it. I want to hear what
you get on this."

"O.K. There are places to start looking. More of the damn routine," said Clock with a scowl. "As if we hadn't enough to do already." He looked at his watch. "I've got to get back too—that Mrs.
Moorhead—Pete, you can do the initial report and talk to some people."

"Not many names in the address book," said Petrovsky. "Try the
bowling alley, that bar down the street. And then there's Gardena."

Jesse cocked his head at them. "I'm just the damn fool civilian
who reads detective stories sometimes. I may be jumping to conclusions, but what I heard from that fellow at The Rink—McAllister
quitting his job because he expected to be getting a bundle of loot—
it doesn't strike you as a possible lead? What about Gardena?"

Clock tossed the matchbox up and caught it. "It occurs to me.
You know the old story, Jesse. The only game in town. Even before
he broke up with the blond, she was working nights to 2 A.M. and
he had to spend his time somewhere."

"I'll go and ask." Petrovsky sounded amused.

"You let me know what shows, Andrew."

"And thanks so much for handing us a new case. All we needed."

◎◎◎

There was more truth than poetry in that. Clock didn't have time
for lunch. He had two cups of coffee over more paper work, back at
the precinct house, and was just finishing a report on the latest burglary when the lab called. They'd lifted some good latents on that
job, and just made them out of their own records downtown: one
Rex Linker, a long pedigree of burglary, B. and E., petty theft, auto
theft. He was currently on parole from Folsom.

"These goddamn punks!" said Clock. You would think anybody'd
have better sense, but of course the punks didn't or they wouldn't be

punks. He got on the phone to Welfare and Rehabilitation down-town, found out who Linker's P.A. officer was, talked to him, took down Linker's address. By the rules, a man on parole had to have a job, and Linker had; he was working at a gas station and living in a rented room four blocks away—he wasn't allowed to drive on P.A. The room was two blocks away from where the burglary had been pulled. "Punks!" said Clock. The P.A. officer said he'd meet him at the station to put the arm on Linker. "Not me, somebody else—I'm busy." Clock looked around to see who was in, and Mantella was typing a report across the office. He sent Mantella to pick up Linker, and three minutes later the desk sergeant called to say Mrs. Moorhead was on her way up.

Clock spent a profitable forty-five minutes with her and the cute, serious little girl named Edna. The fellow who had tried to get Edna into his car, off the public school playground, the other day hadn't realized that Edna's mother was right there in sight, teaching a craft and hobby class to older children but keeping an unobtrusive eye on Edna. She was a sensible, shrewd woman and a good witness, and she looked carefully at the mug shots Clock produced.

"Of course you couldn't go by just what Edna could say about him, I see that, though she's quite mature for her age. And I only got one good look at him, and the car. But I think I'd place him if he's one of these." She studied the shots slowly.

They'd had two cases, last month, two weeks ago, of child molesta-tion, one a real rape, and the girl, seven years old, still in the hospi-tal. From the only description they had—a couple walking their dog who'd heard the girl scream and seen him running away—Clock had picked out seven men from records, men with that kind of history who matched the description roughly. He'd mixed in a few more miscellaneous mug shots at random for Mrs. Moorhead.

She finally singled out two of them, said apologetically, "I can't say definitely, Sergeant, but it could have been either one of these. That one a little more likely, I think. The car I can be positive about, as I said—it was a blue Nova, two-door, about three years old." But she hadn't seen the plate number, so that was no use.

The two shots she had picked out might take them somewhere. William Lightner, forty-three, five-ten, a hundred and forty, brown and blue, pedigree of statutory rape, child molestation, enticement of minors, petty theft. Roy Donahue, thirty-eight, five-nine, a hundred and thirty, brown and blue, pedigree of child molestation, peeping tom, B. and E. Both were out from recent short stretches, not on parole. Look for them, haul them in and lean on them; sometimes the sex nuts came apart without much trouble.

He thanked Mrs. Moorhead and she took Edna away. Mantella came back and said they'd picked up Linker without any fuss and he'd admitted to the burglary when he heard about the prints. He was stashed away. "Another damn report to write," said Clock. And ten to one Linker would get another one-to-three and be out again in three months.

They wouldn't hear anything from the lab on McAllister until tomorrow at least; no autopsy report before Thurday. Funny-peculiar that it should have been Jesse who found him, poking around looking for that blond who'd snatched her own kid. Provisionally Clock didn't think that had anything to do with McAllister getting killed; of course you never knew, but in his experience what a thing looked like was usually what it was, and McAllister looked like the rather simple, straightforward thing to Clock. Academically he wondered what, if anything, the lab would turn up on it.

Josie wasn't feeling so scared and empty inside as a couple of days ago, but she was feeling more plain mad, in an upside-down sort of way. She couldn't remember all Mother Sue had said, but there'd been something about your real mama, of course mamas always want their own children, God puts it in their hearts. And it wasn't so with this one.

Right now she was in there in front of the dressing table getting fixed up to go out, putting on lipstick and black stuff on her eyelashes. She had on a real pretty dress with blue and white flowers on it, a white bead necklace and earrings and high-heeled white sandals. She'd put some light brown makeup on her legs instead of stockings, and the lipstick was bright red. She was pretty, Josie had decided, with her wavy blond hair and the way her face sloped down to a pretty curvy mouth, but it wasn't a nice sort of prettiness because she wasn't nice inside.

The Denny man was sitting in the living room reading a newspaper; he'd turned off the TV. He looked tired and sort of cross too.

Josie went into the bedroom and said directly, "You don't really want me here so I don't see why you had to take me away from home."

Mama looked at her. "Well, aren't we the smarty-pants? You go read a book or something. You stay here as long as I say."

"I've read all my books. There's nothing to do here, and I don't want to stay. I want to go home. I don't see why you want me to stay when you don't even like me," said Josie clearly.

"Shut up," said Mama.

"But there's nothing to do. I'll have to go out sometime, there'll be school starting next month."

"Aw, spit-cat, don't be mean to the kid," said Denny. "You can't keep her cooped up all the time, gossakes, I been feeling like a jailer myself. Listen, you won't be back for a while—I'll take her out to a movie or something, find a place air conditioned, O.K.?"

"I'm not supposed to go to a movie unless Mother Sue says it's all right." Neither of them answered that.

"Come on, kitten, she's just a little kid," said Denny. "And it's so damn hot, that fan don't help much. It'll be O.K."

"Oh, for God's sake," said Mama, "do what you want as long as you get her back here sometime." She put her lipstick and powder puff into her big white handbag and went out to the living room. "Give me the car keys, lover-boy."

"O.K., O.K. Good luck, kitten. Don't worry about us, we'll find some place to go."

"Why should I worry about you?" said Mama, but that time it was like she was smiling, she really liked Denny.

So did Josie, kind of; he wasn't like any grown-up she'd known before, the way he really wanted you to like him, tried to be nice when Mama wasn't. After Mama left, he said to Josie, "What'd you like to do, kid? We look and see what movies are on?"

Josie considered. "I'd like to go to the library," she said. "Is there one close?" The one nearest home was a mile away, and Daddy Fred took them in the car every Friday night, to take the old books back and get new ones.

Denny looked awfully surprised. "The liberry?" he said. "That's a damn funny place for a kid to want to go. I don't know, I'd hafta look it up." He got the phone book and looked and said there was one on Wilshire. She knew that street's name, and small reassurance warmed her suddenly; she wasn't way off somewhere, she knew Daddy Fred drove on Wilshire sometimes, it wasn't anywhere near home or on the way to school but it was still Los Angeles. "We'll hafta take a bus," said Denny.

They went out and walked up the street to a main street. There were a lot of apartments and stores. Josie felt some better just to be out of the apartment, it was a little cooler in the street, but she had on the same panties and socks she'd worn the last three days on account of no clean ones, and her dress was all wrinkled, it wasn't any way to go out, somewhere in a bus, Mother Sue wouldn't like it. Josie didn't know what she'd do about clothes. At home, all the washing was put in the machine Tuesdays and Fridays, but there wasn't a washing machine at the apartment and she didn't know how to run one anyway.

They got on a bus and then walked some more and found the library. It was bigger than the one near home. But Denny, trying to be nice, was really sort of stupid. He didn't know about library cards, and when Josie explained and they asked the woman at the desk, she couldn't give Josie one because Denny wasn't a relative.

"Well, look, never mind, kid," he said. "Hell, you don't want to sit and read books all the time anyway. Hey, I'll bet you're hungry, we better go get some lunch and then look for a movie, you like that?"

They got on another bus and he said they'd go to a place named Lew's, she could have a cheeseburger and he'd have a beer to cool off, it sure was hot. When they got there it wasn't anything like the restaurants Josie'd been to a few times with Daddy Fred and Mother Sue, all light and clean with tablecloths or place mats and a waitress to bring what you wanted. It was dark and not very big and it smelled, and there were a lot of men, no ladies at all. Some of the men knew Denny.

"Hey, buddy-boy, you pickin' 'em outta the cradle?" said one.

"Little young for you, ain't she, Denny?" And another man in a white apron behind a long counter came over and said, "Yipes, Denny, you know you're not supposed bring kids in here. What the hell?"

"Knock it off," said Denny, sounding kind of embarrassed. "Look, I'm just sort of baby-sitting for her mama awhile, Josie's a nice kid. We'll only be here a little while, Joe. You bring her a cheeseburger and I'll have a beer and a ham on rye."

The man hunched his shoulders and went away and brought the lunch. After all the doctor's tests a couple of years ago Josie wasn't supposed to eat any cheese so she scraped that off, but the hamburger wasn't very good, too red, not like Mother Sue's. Denny had some more beers and got talking with some men sitting at the next table; he didn't talk to Josie for a while. She saw a door marked *Ladies* and after a while she went in there, and when she came back Denny was playing cards with the men. He'd forgotten about the movie, but Josie didn't care; she didn't go to movies much, except Disney ones, and there was air conditioning here, real cold and nice after the hot air outside. Pretty soon a man came up and sat at the table with her, one of the men who had joked at Denny, so he knew him. He was a thin man with a long nose and glasses.

"Your date's neglectin' you," he said, smiling at her. "That's a shame. You're too pretty a girl to sit here all alone."

"I'm all right," said Josie.

"My name's Don. You like another hamburger?"

"No, thank you."

"Where'd Denny get hold of a sweet little girl like you? Cat got your tongue? That's sure a pretty dimple you got." He talked like she was about five instead of practically nine, but at least he was friendly, and Josie was polite. He was still there when Denny came back.

"Hey, kid," he said, "hey, I'm sorry, I shouldn't of let the guys talk me into playin'. I don't guess we'd have time to go to a movie now, I'm sorry."

"That's all right," said Josie.

The man in the apron came over and said, "Look Denny, you said just awhile. I lose my license, any cops see a kid in here."

"O.K., O.K.," said Denny. They went out again into the hot

street. "I guess we better get back," said Denny. "She'll be home pretty soon."

For a while there'd been different things to think about; now Josie was thinking about that again. Mama. She didn't want Josie any way at all; she didn't like her even. For a reason Josie couldn't understand she could take her away from home, away from everything, and Daddy Fred and Mother Sue couldn't stop her. Just to keep her, the way Mrs. Underwood across the street kept the little brown dog tied to a stake all the while and Mother Sue said it broke her heart, the poor thing neglected so— Not like Bix, who had a whole big yard to play in, the fence so he couldn't get out and get hurt, and Daddy Fred took him on walks, with Josie going along—

For the first time, walking along the hard hot pavement beside Denny, Josie had the blinding thought: If they don't want me, why do I have to stay? Why can't I just go home?

It was still Los Angeles, home was somewhere here. If she knew which way she could walk—if she could get away. Mama not there a lot of the time, but Denny there, and he was nice to her but she knew he'd stop her trying to get away. She hadn't any money. She'd had nearly two dollars saved up out of her allowance, in the pretty gold bag she carried to Sunday school, buy it hadn't got put in the suitcase. You had to pay on a bus, but there were taxi cabs. When Ruthie Graham's grandmother came to visit from back east she took a taxi cab from the airport because Mr. Graham's car wasn't working, and it cost seven dollars, but you didn't pay till you got there. And the name would be in the phone book, you just phoned and asked for one. It might cost more than seven dollars, and Daddy Fred had been worried about money lately, but he'd pay—if the taxi cab brought her home—

To get home—suddenly Josie shivered and sighed. "You O.K., kid?" asked Denny. Josie didn't answer him. It had just occurred to her, she knew where home was of course—532 Kingsley Avenue— but she didn't know where the apartment was. What street or anything.

She tried to look at the signs on the next corner, but Denny was hurrying, pulling her along, and as they turned down the side street she got just one look at the black and white sign. Adams, it said, and that was the name of the main street, not this one.

⊚⊚⊚

"Well, it looked all kosher to me," said Lorna. "The papers and so on. I think it's level, Mr. Quiller."

"Jesus," he said. "I'll tell you one thing for true, baby. Little old Stevie ain't handing out any bread without Vic's say-so in black and white. You know what I mean? I do a thing like that all on my own, uh-uh. Any figures mentioned maybe?"

"Fifty G's," said Lorna.

"Oh, ouch, could be worse, but I ain't about to pay out fifty cents and expect to collect it back from Vic because he owed it. No way. And, for Chrissakes, look at this damn thing!" He waved the yellow sheet at her. "I thought we were living in the age of progress and culture, for Chrissakes. Western Union saying they can't deliver a cable to this Godforsaken spot—I ask you, what the hell do I do? Stall?"

Lorna regarded him thoughtfully. "Not very long, Mr. Quiller. At what they call an educated guess."

"Like that. You'd know. Damn it, why'd I ever get into this god-damned business?" It was a cry from the heart.

⊚⊚⊚

Clock had gone out looking for Lightner and then Donahue; one like that they wanted off the streets. Both addresses out of records were n.g. Mostly they had to do it the hard way. Lightner was an experienced electrician, Donahue had worked as a trucker, plumber, janitor. Put out the A.P.B.'s and see if they could turn them up. He'd just got back to the office and done that, at five-fifteen, when Petrovsky came in. Clock brought him up to date on the various cases on hand and asked, "What did you turn on McAllister?"

"This and that, for a first cast." Petrovsky sat down, loosening his tie, and lit a cigarette. "I saw some people out of the address book. Mrs. Lisa Adler, husband used to work with McAllister at another bowling alley. Last time they saw him was about two and a half weeks ago when his girl friend passed out at a party there and he was annoyed. Bob Klingman, bartender at that place down from The

Rink, he said McAllister dropped in a few times a week, never had more than a couple of beers. Davenport, the owner—a little pay dirt. He says he knew McAllister was a gambler, a few times he'd asked for a salary advance, got burned in a game. Davenport thought he was a fool, admitted he couldn't complain about his work but said—how true, how true—that any man given to playing cards for money, not the best fellow to be taking any charge of your money. I asked about that at the bar—Klingman very cagey, sometimes a few regulars had a little hand of gin, just for fun, no money."

"Naturally," said Clock.

"He didn't seem to know anybody else at the hotel but Archer. He'd been living there since February. I haven't," said Petrovsky, "got to Gardena yet."

"Tomorrow. If we have time, and nothing else comes up. The lab may turn something."

Petrovsky stretched out his short legs. "It wasn't a pro takeoff, Andrew."

"Anything but. Mark suddenly suspecting a run of luck, and sore, more likely."

"And he wasn't the slick pro sure-thing man. Working a regular job, which they seldom do."

"Figure it," said Clock. "That was a new deck, Pete."

"Oh, yes," said Petrovsky. "I noticed."

◎◎◎

Jesse fidgeted around the living room after dinner until Nell told him he was driving her wild. "Sorry," said Jesse humbly. "It's just, I once took a course in logic in college."

"What's that got to do with your wearing out the carpet?"

"Simplicities," said Jesse. "I don't know if it applies in real life. Something like the shortest distance between two points. When two unusual occurrences take place within the same orbit, so to speak—to the same set of people—the economics of logic say they're connected."

"McAllister," said Nell. "It is funny, but—"

"Not that overworked word," said Jesse. He wandered down the hall, pursued by Athelstane, and consulted his notebook for the number. Athelstane was fascinated by the telephone, and sat on his feet to listen. "Mrs. Lefkowitz? Just checking to see if you're at home. Few more questions to ask if you don't mind."

"Playing detective," said Nell as he put on his jacket. "You'd much better leave it to Andrew."

At the old apartment building on Manhattan Place, Christine Lefkowitz let him in reluctantly, didn't invite him to sit down. "I don't know what else I can tell you," she said sharply. She had a black nylon-jersey robe belted around her good figure.

Jesse couldn't have said why he felt, for no good reason at all, that she knew something about Nonie she hadn't told him. About Nonie, about what?

It was—the places people lived said this and that about them—a typical sort of living room, the vintage of this kind of apartment. Worn beige carpeting, matching overstuffed couch and chair also beige, the modern TV in one corner would be hers, rose-beige drapes, uninspired anonymous dim landscape in a gilt frame on one wall. Christine not the homebody, concerned for the interior décor.

"I thought you'd be interested to know," he said, "that Roger McAllister is dead. Apparently murdered."

She stared at him, and her white skin suddenly took on a greenish tint; her eyes widened to show the whites. She stepped back, nearly stumbling, and leaned on the overstuffed chair. "My God!" she said. At least he had an answer of sorts here: that had rocked her like a body blow, that she hadn't expected. "McAllister? M—oh, my God! But how—I mean, who—"

"Investigation going on. I just happen to know the officer in charge of the case," said Jesse, watching her. "You have any ideas about it?"

"Me?" She had recovered herself at once; she laughed rather shrilly, found a pack of cigarettes on the end table, lit one with the lighter beside it. "What would I know about it? He was never any friend of mine. Nonie's boy friend for a while, but she broke up with him a couple of weeks—a month—ago. I never knew him."

"Oh, she'd definitely broken up with him, you knew that. You didn't mention that before."

"Well, she had. Something she said—why should I mention it?

My God, that's a terrible thing, him getting killed, but it's nothing to do with Nonie. Or, for God's sake, me."

"It doesn't really look that way. Maybe the police figure different. I just thought you'd be interested."

She gave him a cold look and said, "Not very. And if you'll excuse me, I put in a long day, I'm tired."

Going down the thin-carpeted stairs, Jesse thought, Damn, I wish I knew what old Edgar would say about all this.

FIVE

It was more of the usual tedious routine, along with all the other cases they had on hand to work. Glorified clerks, thought Clock, facing more paper work on Wednesday morning. And there were always the details. The corpses, however they got to be corpses, had to be tidied away, and where possible they liked to find somebody to pay for the funeral besides the taxpayers.

The night attendant at The Rink had said that McAllister once mentioned he was from Kansas City, and among the addresses in the book found on him was that of a Mrs. Phyllis Kramer in Kansas City, Missouri. Clock got on the phone to the K.C. force and talked to a Captain Longworth, who said genially they'd send somebody there to break the news and ask questions. Somebody would get back to Clock.

Petrovsky had gone down to Gardena to start that routine. Clock might have gone to join him—that could be a long piece of work—but as he put the phone down Detective Guttierez came in with one of the suspects in another burglary, and Clock helped out on the questioning. They didn't get anything definite, finally let him go, and then Clock got around to looking at the reports the night watch had left: another burglary, two more heists and an assault with intent. They had put out an A.P.B. on that one for one Byron Lampier, an ex-con with a hasty temper, and sent an inquiry up to D.M.V. about a car; the answer had come back after the night watch went off, so now Clock added that to the A.P.B., an old Buick sedan, the plate number. He wondered how Petrovsky was doing.

Petrovsky, philosophically used to the plodding routine, had had worse jobs. The reason, of course, that both he and Clock had thought of Gardena was the curious oversight of that gaggle of politicians a while ago. It was illegal to gamble in the state of California, except inside the race tracks and specified places with proper licenses; and in drawing up the tight lists against it, the politicians had outlawed every known game of chance except draw poker. In the city of Gardena, adjacent suburb to L.A., flourished all the licensed gambling houses.

If McAllister had been a steady gambler, he'd probably be known somewhere down here. These places were tightly and honestly run, no funny stuff: they didn't need to be crooked to take a profit, supplying the food and drink, cards and chips, at a price; and while there'd be drifters in and out, most of the regular customers would have favorite spots and be known. And all of these places were open twenty-four hours a day.

He started out methodically with the biggest. He had a shot of McAllister blown up from the I.D. photo on his license. At the first, second and third places he drew blank, but at the fourth he talked to the manager, who happened to be in early, who looked at the blow-up and said, "Yes, I know him. He's in here pretty regular."

"Alone, or with the same pals, or what?" asked Petrovsky. These houses in a way could be compared to gents' clubs or those old coffee houses: gathering places for lonely men, men with time on their hands. Some of them would come in groups, buddies already known, for a few friendly hands; some would come alone, meet new buddies or join a hand with strangers. "And how often?"

The manager was still looking at the blow-up. "Four, five nights a week the last couple of years. Quiet fellow, never any trouble. He came alone at first, but since then he's joined a couple of regular groups, six-seven-eight fellows come in about the same times. I don't know any names. They all look like the ordinary upright citizens, the decent jobs—a few drinks, nothing out of line." These places were always vigilant for anything out of line.

"He'd been playing just with that one bunch lately?"

"I'm not here twenty-four hours a day. I'd seen him with other men too, nights none of those was here, but if any of them was, he was usually with them, played with them oftener. A couple of them are older men, the rest about his age."

"Who might know any names?" asked Petrovsky.

"Possibly one of the waiters. These people are so damn super-stitious, favorite tables and so on, that bunch usually sits at one of the front tables by the right window, and that'd be Herbert's station. No, I don't gamble," said the manager seriously to Petrovsky's mute look. "Few people who work in gambling houses do. Herbert's not on till two, but I can get you his address."

Herbert Leeds' address was in Watts, a neatly kept single frame house; Leeds was about forty, tall and thin and not very black, and he was co-operative. "Yes, sir, I know this gentleman," he said to the blow-up. "The fellows he plays with regular? Different ones, but you see, with the gentlemen come in pretty often, they'll meet up with each other oftenest and end up at one table. There's this little crowd generally in weekends, some nights this gentleman sat in with. I couldn't tell you but two names, sir. A Mr. Gebhart, they call him Howie, and a Mr. James Morrison. I think Mr. Morrison works at Lockheed."

None of those names had been in McAllister's address book. Pe-trovsky found a phone and got on to Lockheed. By eleven o'clock he was talking to Morrison, who was in personnel there. Morrison was in his mid-thirties, a ready talker, interested to meet a detective.

"I've always liked cards as a relaxation," he said. "I got in the habit of dropping down there a couple of nights a week when I first landed here. I didn't know a soul in L.A." He agreed that there was this group that generally played together, if two or more of them happened to be there; McAllister had been one. "Though he played with other men too, I know he was there a lot more than the rest of us. It's just the way it happened, whoever was there when." He had seemed to be a nice guy; Morrison didn't know much about him. There were about six other men who usually gravitated together if they were there at the same time—"Not all at once, you know"—and Morrison only knew them casually. Lee Bryant, Howard Geb-hart, Wilfred Shotwell, Johnny Hope. With thought he dredged up two more, Chuck King and Jim Noble. From the casual talk he could tell Petrovsky about jobs, no addresses. Gebhart worked for a supermarket chain, Bryant for Sears, Hope had just opened his own gunsmith's shop, King was in public relations, a Hollywood agency, he didn't know which.

That was enough to go on with. Petrovsky evaded more questions about McAllister and started back to the office.

Captain Longworth called Clock back at eleven-thirty. "This Mrs. Kramer turned out to be your corpse's sister. We told her to call you collect. No trouble, glad to oblige. How's the weather out there? It's hot as hell here."

Clock said it was the same in California. Five minutes later Phyllis Kramer called, and he swore mentally when she said her name; he never knew what to say to sorrowing relations. But it seemed she wasn't sorrowing all that much; she said in a thin voice, "Well, he hadn't been home in years, since Mother and Dad were killed in the accident. I don't suppose he had much money, Sergeant."

"We've found about nine hundred dollars." McAllister had had a checking account at a bank near the hotel. "There'll be a little red tape, but if you're the closest relative—"

"Oh. Well, I don't see any sense in bringing him back here. Could you tell me what I'd better do?"

"I can put you in touch with a local undertaker, arrange for the body to be sent there."

"That's what we'd better do," she said. She didn't ask many questions about the murder.

Clock had time for lunch today; when he got back Petrovsky was in and told him what had showed. They were both on the phone, trying to run down some of those other men, when a couple of uniformed men came in with Byron Lampier; they'd spotted the plate number from the A.P.B. In this busy precinct station, the detectives were used to switching from case to case. Clock left Petrovsky on the phone; he and Mantella spent an hour talking to Lampier, who finally came apart and gave them a statement, and Clock took him down to the Alameda jail and booked him in.

When he got back Petrovsky was typing a report. "We just got one of our bodies identified at least. Missing Persons sent a female up just after you left. Daughter missing since Sunday. Her all right. Feeble sort of soul, don't know what young people are coming to. I had to tell her it was an O.D. She gave me a couple of names, girl friends, boy friends."

"Not that it'll ever come to anything," said Clock. "Charge of abandoning a body, if we could ever pin it down. Did you locate any of the happy gamblers?"

"Addresses for Bryant and Gebhart. Gebhart's not home and the market says it's his day off."

"That'll do for today," said Clock. It was two-fifty then.

Lee Bryant was a department manager at the big Sears warehouse out on Western; when Clock showed him the badge, mentioned McAllister, he got flustered and excited. "Murdered!" he said. "My God, who killed him? Then maybe Howie was right, he was a real criminal of some kind. I'll be damned." He was a stocky man in his mid-thirties, sandy and round-faced.

"Right about what?" asked Clock. "Can we talk here, Mr. Bryant?"

"Yes, sure, I'm the boss here—come into my office, I'll get another chair— Well, you see, Sergeant, this McAllister sat in with a kind of regular bunch of us, a couple times a week, down at this place in Gardena like you said. You know how it goes, win a hand, lose a hand, no sweat. We don't play big stakes, all friendly together."

"You and this Gebhart, King, Shotwell—a few others. Any of you know each other before?"

"No, we just sort of fell in together—me and Howie and Johnny Hope to start. They're all nice guys, level, it's not a big thing, way to pass time. Howie's a lot older than the rest of us but a very good guy, solid. Like I say, we'd win a few, lose a few, nobody was getting rich or poor at it, and there's such a thing as a run of luck. I know about six months ago Howie had a real hot run, he couldn't lose, must have run it up to three, four hundred bucks before it quit on him. Happens to anybody. But just lately McAllister was winning hot and heavy, and just last week Howie said to me and Johnny he suspected he was cheating some way. He wasn't—McAllister—any more than a middling player, and he sure hadn't had any such run of luck with us before. Well, I mean, you don't expect a thing like that, ordinary friendly guys you been playing with, I said to Howie he must be wrong, and Johnny said it was the hell of a run McAllister had going anyway and he wouldn't say Howie was wrong—"

"Do you know how much either of them might have dropped to McAllister?"

Bryant shrugged. "A hundred, seventy-five. I was down about sixty. It was the principle of the thing, Sergeant—that was what Howie said. Nobody wants a dirty thing like that. We all felt a little dirty even talking about it, thinking it could be. But Howie was mad. It wasn't just the money, the principle of the thing."

"Had you decided to do anything about it? You could have got him outlawed from play down there."

"There wasn't any proof. How could we be sure, that's what I said to Howie—for God's sake, none of us experts at card cheats and how they do it. The hell of it was"—he wrinkled his forehead at Clock—"you can see how it was. Say I'd drop in there, like Friday night after work, Howie'd be there or Johnny, or Noble, *or* McAllister, and we'd say hello, how goes it, order a beer and sit down. And after all that, how in hell—like I said to Howie—are we going to get out of playing with him? If he's there? Without coming out and accusing him, and there wasn't any proof."

"Gebhart was mad," said Clock.

"Damn right. And if he was right, I don't blame him. So was I."

"You come to any conclusion? Going to ignore McAllister, stop playing with him, bring it out in the open?"

"We hadn't decided, no. But now he's dead—my God, that is a thing, a guy you know murdered—you don't know who? How'd it happen?"

"We're not sure yet," said Clock. "Thanks, Mr. Bryant, you've been a help." Sometimes the tedious routine offered shortcuts.

◎◎◎

On Thursday morning the autopsy report came in, and Clock read it with some interest. "There you are," he said to Petrovsky. "Short and sweet. Just as I said, no lady accounted for McAllister—and he was temporarily off women anyway, after the fight with the blond." McAllister had actually died of strangulation, but his neck had been broken too and he'd been beaten up some. Together with the lab evidence on the car, in or near the car, more probably in it. Bruise on left side of the jaw, temple and cheek. Lacerations on right hand; he'd fought back, may have marked the other fellow. Bruises on throat, hyoid bone crushed; and marks on the window ledge on the driver's side of the Study suggested that he'd been forced back and held down there strongly enough, probably during the strangulation, to break his neck. Estimated time of death, between midnight last Friday night and midnight Saturday night; the weather hadn't helped them pin it down. "He was a big man," said Clock. "Young, in reasonably good condition. It took another to do that."

"Or somebody," said Petrovsky, "damn mad at him."

"Or both. Let's get out of here before anything new goes down."

They found Gebhart at his job; he was the manager of a chain market in Monterey Park. He looked at the badges with interest, said Lee Bryant had called him last night and took them to a cubbyhole of an office a few steps above the main floor of the market, where a complicated arrangement of mirrors afforded an exaggerated view of all the aisles and shoppers. After a few minutes Clock turned his back on that; it made him dizzy.

"Now this is quite a thing, a murder," said Gebhart. "Lee told you what I'd been thinking about McAllister. A hell of a thing." He sat squarely in the armless vinyl-padded chair before a tiny desk, dwarfing both; he was a big barrel-chested man in the late fifties or early sixties, nearly bald, with a bulldog's face and beefy hands. "Damn it, I never was one to gamble much—but one way and another I'd just got in the habit of going down there, the last couple of years. I suppose it was not having enough to do, after Bill got transferred. Seems like I was always busy some way, before Annie—my wife—died, things around the house, walking the dog, all like that. And Bill, our son, he lived right down in Santa Monica with June and the two kids, they'd be up to see us or we'd be there, and I never had any spare time off the job. Then Annie went with a heart attack —I wouldn't know which is worse, have it happen sudden or slow— and the old dog didn't last long after her, and last year Bill got transferred to Seattle, he works for Boeing, and there I was. Nobody at home, nobody to go and see. Oh, we had friends, sure, and they'd ask me to dinner, but you don't want to take advantage. I've never been one for reading or the TV, I didn't know what to do with myself, and upshot was I got in the habit of going down there for a few hands of draw."

"And met some new friends," said Clock.

"Sure. All nice fellows, if most of 'em younger than me. Just ordi-

nary fellows looking to relax a little over a friendly game. And then
that had to happen. We must've been playing with McAllister, on
and off, nearly a year. It was only lately I got suspicious he was having too many runs of luck—it wasn't natural."

"And according to Bryant you were mad," said Petrovsky.

"You're damn right I was!" The veins swelled in Gebhart's thick
neck and his face reddened a little. "We didn't play high stakes, but
it adds up. I went back over my records—I always keep records of everything just for my own satisfaction—and that joker'd taken me for
nearly four hundred bucks in the last four months. You're damn
right I was mad."

"So what did you do about it, Mr. Gebhart?" asked Clock.

Gebhart looked from one to the other of them. "Do about it?
Why, I'd made up my mind not to play with him again, and if anything was said about it I'd tell him why, plain out."

"You didn't tackle him directly about it?"

"I hadn't seen him since last week."

"Did you know where he lived?"

"As a matter of fact I did. He mentioned it one time. What are
you getting at?"

"So tell us," said Petrovsky, "where you were last Friday and Saturday nights, Mr. Gebhart."

"Me?" said Gebhart. All of a sudden he saw where this was head-
ing, and he lowered his head like a bull and glowered at them. "You
got some fool idea that I murdered him? Me? You asking me for an
alibi?"

"If you've got one."

"Well, for God's sake, I haven't. I wouldn't kill a man over four
hundred dollars."

"As Mr. Bryant quoted you, it was the principle of the thing," said
Clock.

"Well, my God, it was. The damn dirty crook—not like he was
cheating millionaires at Monte Carlo, just decent ordinary working
men looking for a little entertainment. That's crazy," said Gebhart,
"me kill anybody."

"What about Friday and Saturday?" asked Clock.

"What in hell can I tell you? I work nine to six. I just didn't feel like poker since all that last week, I didn't go anywhere but home. It's a single house, I don't know if the neighbors could say I was there. Both days. I had a couple of beers, fixed dinner and went to bed." He was looking apprehensive now. "You aren't serious, are you? Thinking it was me killed him?"

◎◎◎

"Are we serious about it, Pete?" asked Clock in the Pontiac.

"Half and half. He could have done it in a temper. Got to brooding on the principle, gone down there to tackle McAllister, they had a row and bingo. It could also have been one of the others, or somebody we haven't heard of yet McAllister had also taken."

"And there probably won't be much to say one way or the other." Clock started the car. Back at the station, they found all the interrogation rooms occupied: three burglary suspects, one rape suspect under questioning. Maybe a few current cases would get written off; but new ones were always coming along.

Petrovsky went back to Gardena to try to turn up some more names. Clock started going over the night-watch reports.

At three-thirty Jesse called. "I could bear to hear what's shown up on McAllister," he said. "You left me cliff-hanging."

"Preserve patience. I was just about to call my wife and tell her we'll go out to dinner, some place air conditioned. We'll be up about eight if you haven't anything else to do."

"I hope to God you're not going to tie Nonie into it. On the other hand— *The way of man is froward and strange,* so says Solomon, and I sometimes think you can double it in spades for woman. I just do not understand that girl. Yes, well, we'll expect you, Andrew."

◎◎◎

"It all looks pretty straightforward, up to a point," said Clock. He was comfortably full of dinner and feeling somnolent, relaxed on the couch; the air conditioning was on full. It had gone up to a hundred and three today, with a smog alert. Jesse was sitting opposite, feeding pretzels to Athelstane, the two girls curled up in opposite chairs.

"That deck of readers was the giveaway, and everything followed the way Pete and I read it."

"Specialized knowledge." Fran nodded her neat dark head. "At least it's a relief to know Nonie isn't mixed up in a murder. I've been worrying about that poor little girl."

"What Jesse's come up with, maybe she's having the time of her life," said Nell. "We'll come to that later. What about McAllister, Andrew?"

"Oh, we heard from all over about his fight with the girl friend. Evidently he was full of it a couple of weeks ago—he'd mentioned it to a lot of people. Well, he wasn't the pro gambler, the sure-thing man living by his wits. He had a regular job, but it was peanuts. He was just getting along, the very ordinary fellow, very ordinary life, and of course driving that broken-down old clunker, and he wanted a lot more. He'd been dropping down to Gardena to play poker, probably just for something to do at first, and then just lately, I don't know how lately, he decided to use it for something more. As I told Jesse, there are business firms that sell all that equipment, marked cards, hold-out boxes, all the stock in trade of the crooked gamblers. They don't advertise in respectable magazines, but they're available. He may have come across an ad, the fine-print classified in a tabloid or somewhere, sent for those readers—we'll probably never know. And he wouldn't have been an expert—that's a damn hard way to make a living—but it was enough to give him an edge in an honest game. He'd started winning oftener than he lost, and I'd guess he had the feeling, how long has this been going on? Easy money. So far as we know he hadn't been playing with men who went for high stakes, but it would add up. I'd have a further guess that when he quit that two-bit job last week, and let it slip that he'd be taking more loot than the job was worth, he was planning to go into gambling full time, with his little gimmicks to give him the edge."

"Oh," said Nell, disappointed. "I thought that sounded as if he was blackmailing somebody."

Clock smiled at her indulgently. "Real life tends to be simpler than books. He'd have found out it isn't as easy as it looked, you know. But just at first, the money coming in pretty steady, it looked to him like a wonderful lay. Only he used the gimmicks too often, he was winning too steady from the same men and a couple of them got suspicious." He told them about Bryant, about Gebhart. "There are probably others we haven't tracked down, but right now I'm thinking Gebhart could be X. He was sore about the money, but even more about being fooled. He could have brooded on it, gone to tackle McAllister about it, lost his temper."

"How did McAllister come to be in his car?" asked Jesse.

"We'll likely never know all the ins and outs, unless Gebhart—or another X—tells us. You can use imagination. Say Gebhart was waiting for him in that parking lot Saturday night when he got home. He probably knew McAllister's car. Went over and spoke to him, got in the car. They had a row. Gebhart went for McAllister, and McAllister couldn't have fought back very well if he was behind the wheel—that would give Gebhart the edge. He's a powerful man, if a lot older than McAllister. If it was Gebhart, I doubt if he meant to kill the man—he was just mad, and it was done in a minute, it doesn't take long to kill a man that way. And when he saw McAllister was dead, he just dumped him in the back seat with some vague idea of delaying discovery, and took off."

"Fine full-blood-and-thunder imagining," said Jesse.

"And I'll tell you now, I doubt we'll ever charge anybody for that kill. There's no possible case against Gebhart. He could have done it, Bryant could have done it, anybody who was sore about McAllister cheating him. I think it's in the cards Gebhart did it, but there's no real evidence. There's only one little thing I don't like about that reading of it," said Clock, "and it's a niggling little thing that may not matter a damn."

"What?" asked Nell interestedly.

"The steering wheel and dashboard were wiped clean of any latents. Polished clean. The rest of the car was dirty. And anybody who reads detective stories might have done that."

"Gebhart might have done it," said Jesse, "when he snapped out of his temper and realized what he'd done."

"Exactly," said Clock. "It's nothing. I think it's more likely McAllister was killed Saturday night—Archer saw him come in at midnight on Friday, he's not apt to have gone out again. But it's six of one, half dozen of the other."

"Anyway Nonie didn't do it," said Fran. "Have you got anywhere on Nonie, Jesse?"

"Playing detective," said Jesse. "I don't know what I've got. I don't understand females."

"I don't understand this one," said Nell, "if that is Nonie you just got a sniff of. Oh, damn, there's the baby—I'll go—you tell them, Jesse."

◎◎◎

Yesterday morning Jesse had wasted an hour in court, on another divorce hearing, only to have the judge succumb to an incubating virus and leave the bench before eleven. He hadn't any appointments the Gordons couldn't handle, a lot of paper work he could be doing, but he didn't feel inclined to go back to the office.

And he wasn't thinking so much about Nonie, in this queer case, as about Josie. Snatched, Clock said. A legal kidnapping; so it was, in a way. Nonie for whatever reason deciding she wanted Josie back, and what he did know—the little he did know—about fly-by-night, impulsive, fun-time-girl Nonie, he couldn't help wondering what kind of time Josie was having with her. The Lannings serious, upright, God-fearing people; Josie a serious-looking little girl, brought up in the straight and narrow way. What was Josie making of Nonie, and vice versa?

Over a cup of coffee at a drugstore in the Civic Center, he ruminated about that Pierce. Was there any way to chase him down, find out if Nonie had gone off with him or not?

All he knew about Pierce, all anybody at that club knew, was that he liked the topless dancers, went there a lot, was hot for Nonie, was possibly a car salesman and he'd asked Nonie to go on a Caribbean cruise. No guessing where Pierce lived or worked. But if he'd been thinking about a cruise, he might have consulted a travel agency.

There were a lot of those around, and without knowing the area Pierce normally frequented, it would be eeny-meeny-miney-mo. But try a couple of casts anyway, the biggest ones.

Jesse consulted the Yellow Pages and picked three, not arbitrarily. Each of them was a nationwide outfit, and each of the local offices was located somewhere reasonably close to an Automobile Row, a string of agencies. San Vicente, La Cienega, Exposition Boulevard.

At the first one he drew a blank. Nobody remembered Pierce, and by their records nobody by that name had recently bought any tickets. At the second place nobody was anxious to help him, and it took some persuasion before an indolent fat girl looked over their records. No Pierce. At the third place he approached a severely good-looking brunette with horn-rimmed glasses who was one of those naturally efficient females. Her name, on a wooden plaque on her desk, was Anita Reising.

"Afraid I can't tell you any more than that, come close to any date. But you'll have records, if you—"

She had listened, smooth dark head on one side, her brown eyes bright as a robin's. "I'll look it up for you to be sure, sir, but I do remember. As soon as you said the name Pierce. I talked to him myself. Excuse me, is he a friend of yours?"

"Never laid eyes on him." Slightly incredulous, Jesse gave her a card. "Just looking into something for a client. He was in here, the same one you think?"

"By the way you described him. You're a lawyer—it's a divorce case, maybe? Not that I'm asking," and she gave him a mischievous smile. "You didn't strike me as a likely friend of Mr. Pierce's is all. He's a very loud man, you know—if it's the same one—the kind of man who calls anything female 'honeybunch' and 'sweetie-pie,' and you have to watch his hands. Half the time they don't mean any harm, it's just automatic with that kind."

"I know the type. When was he here?"

"It was either Monday or Tuesday two weeks ago, somewhere around the fifth, first week of the month anyway. He was interested in a three-week Caribbean cruise, and he bought two tickets, a double cabin, on the *Princess Pat*. William Pierce, no missus mentioned."

"Two," said Jesse. "No airline tickets to wherever the cruise started?"

"Miami. No, I asked him about it but he said he wasn't sure when they'd want to go, maybe a few days before the cruise started and he'd get them later. He could have got those directly at the airline office, of course."

"This cruise," said Jesse. "When to when?"

"It's one of our nicest package deals," said Miss Reising. "Expensive but everything first-class, and the *Princess Pat*'s one of that line's newest liners. It starts from Miami and goes all around the Caribbean, with a stopover at Nassau, through the Bahamas down to Puerto Rico with stopovers at San Juan and Santo Domingo, to Jamaica with a stopover at Kingston, and then back to Miami by way of New Orleans. There are cruises leaving every week in the season. Three weeks, nineteen hundred and fifty per person."

"Piece of change," said Jesse respectfully. "When did Pierce want to leave?"

"He got tickets on the one leaving a week ago today, the *Princess Pat*, as I said. A double cabin. It's due back in Miami two weeks from today."

Jesse digested that. The girls at the club had said nobody would turn down that invitation; could Nonie have resisted the *Princess Pat*? Nassau and Jamaica? "A double cabin," he said ruminatively. "Tell me, suppose there was a child going along—half fare, or what?"

She looked surprised. "A child? He didn't say anything about—well, if the child was under twelve it would be half fare, but if he'd wanted another cabin—"

Nonie swooping and snatching, thought Jesse. On impulse? Influenced by Rena Sawyer's burgeoning maternal reflections? And that was a week ago on Saturday, Sunday—nearly two weeks ago actually. Pierce had already got the tickets for the cruise. A loud, simple, crude, generous man. "Suppose it came up at the last minute," said Jesse. "Wanting to take the child along. He didn't say anything about who was going with him?"

"No, I assumed—well, that it was his wife, though he doesn't look married, but you never know. Yes, I could tell you about that, oddly enough it came up just the other day, a couple who had tickets for a cruise on the same line, they suddenly decided to take their little boy, and they were able to arrange it on board at the last minute, a cot in one of the stewardess's cabins. The man came in afterward to tell us how accommodating they'd been."

"Um," said Jesse. "Did Pierce give you a check or what?"

"It was a BankAmericard."

"Oh. So you don't have an address for him." It would take Clock's

status, or a court order, to get the credit-card people to part with an
address.

Miss Reising looked suddenly thoughtful. "You know, I do," she
said. "If I can lay a hand on it. Because he gave me a card."

"And I don't suppose you wanted it," said Jesse, "but be a good
girl and try to think what you did with it. You didn't throw it away?
You're so damned efficient, those desk drawers are probably in abso-
lute order and you wouldn't clutter them up with extraneous paper.
Why'd he give you a card?"

Miss Reising laughed. "Well, I didn't want it. He told me he was a
car salesman—I could have guessed—and if I ever was in the market
for a car, new or used, just come see him—all their used cars abso-
lutely the best bargains, reconditioned to the last nut and bolt, satisfaction guaranteed—"

"The warning rattle in fact."

"Just come see him, he'd pick me out a winner. Big Boy they
called him. And he gave me a card. And the desk drawers aren't all
that tidy, I push things in to keep it neat on the surface."

"So you'll look."

She looked, and brought out miscellany, sorting through it; after
ten minutes' search she produced a card, and Jesse received it gratefully. It said *William (Big Boy) Pierce, Dover Motors, Exposition
Boulevard.*

"Same like Rabbi Jeshu ben Sirah says, *Forsake not a wise and
good woman, for her grace is above gold.* Very much obliged, Miss
Reising."

She laughed. "Is it a divorce case?"

"I'm not sure," said Jesse, "just what kind of case it is."

"So you see," said Nell, coming back into the living room, "they
could all be on the cruise together. Having a fine time. Did you tell
them about Mr. Dover?"

"No," said Jesse. He sounded dissatisfied. "Dover owns the car
agency. Ford. Prosperous, polished fellow around forty. He asked if it
was a divorce case too. Pierce is his wife's brother. He all but admitted he carried the fellow out of family feeling, Pierce is a hell of a

good salesman, way he put it, but has to be sat on not to make the hard sell—pushy, brash. Which we had gathered. Said Pierce is always chasing some dame, plays the field. I asked him if Pierce had said anything about this cruise, if he was taking a female along, and Dover laughed and said all he'd heard, Pierce had a cute blond chick lined up to go with him, but no names mentioned. Pierce wouldn't have said anything to Mrs. Dover, she's strait-laced."

"All up in the air," said Clock. "But the fun-time cruise, and the kid?"

"Pierce," said Nell, "doesn't exactly sound like the fatherly type, of course you can bring the kiddie, honey, all have a good time together. But as I said to Jesse, both Pierce and Nonie sound like the kind—doing what comes naturally. Simple. On the whole good-natured. They could have."

"In which case," said Jesse, "we'll just have to wait until they get back." And then he sat up and said, "Damnation. Am I getting slow on the uptake? I just saw that."

"What?" asked Fran.

"And does it say anything? People do move. To cut down on rent, improve the amenities. Why did Nonie, just then? If she was just going on the temporary cruise?"

"I don't think," said Fran, "there's any logical way to reason out why girls like Nonie do anything. They don't operate by any reason. You might get better results consulting Mr. MacDonald, Jesse." Her voice was half serious.

Clock made a derisive noise. "Jesse's ghost factory."

"You ungrateful slob," said Fran. "I have great faith in Mr. Mac-Donald, and you just don't know what you're talking about, Andrew. After what he did for you—" That serious and solemn psychic Mac-Donald had turned up some odd leads a while ago, to clear Clock of that peculiar frame: but of course the old man Edgar Walters had helped on that too.

"If you'd just take the time to read some of the solid evidence, Andrew," said Jesse mildly. "Cops have to know about evidence, same as lawyers—"

"Oh, and I haven't told you about the British colonel," Nell was saying to Fran. "Delicious. He just wrote in his diary—"

"Your dumb blond," said Clock, "will come back eventually. Off the cruise or whatever. Complete with child. Funny as that setup is —but people do funny things, Jesse."

"You tell me nothing," said Jesse fretfully, and fed Athelstane another pretzel.

SIX

He was reluctant to face the Lannings when they came in by invitation late on Friday morning. He had been solidly busy for two and a half hours, not a minute to consider what to say to them. The D.A.'s office had been on the phone; there was definitely going to be prosecution, which was gratifying. The Gorman woman had been in to sign the new will, and a couple of new clients, Mr. and Mrs. Knapp, who took up some time, probably for nothing.

"I mean, Mr. Falkenstein, it's not as if they were friends—bare acquaintances, it was really almost a courtesy call because they'd talked about a room addition to Frank—give him a card, Frank—and really it's a very awkward entrance to the house, all those little brick steps and nothing like an adequate light. And the doctor said my ankle'll be in a cast two months at least and possibly more surgery, and of course we don't have any insurance and really it seems as if they ought to pay my expenses at least, Frank talked to them but they weren't at all nice about it—"

He'd just seen them out when Dangerfield called. "Some more of the red tape. I need a couple of signatures, could you drop in this afternoon about three?"

"Oh, hell," said Jesse unhappily. Dangerfield was the attorney who was seeing the Walters will through probate. "I suppose the rest of them will be there too. All the bureaucrats' paper work. I'd just as soon not run into any of them." He didn't feel exactly guilty about the old man's two sons, daughters-in-law, grandchildren; just disinclined to have to exchange the meaningless amenities—they would be so polite to him, so distant.

"Any trouble?" asked the other attorney.

"No trouble. I didn't approve of the funeral," said Jesse dismally. Such conventional people. A very solemn funeral, and he suspected they'd put up a solid cement tombstone. The old boy would have been annoyed at the waste of money. "I'll stop by on my way home, say five-thirty, O.K.?"

"Anytime," said Dangerfield. "The family will be here at three. You know the red tape, but this is about the last of it, probate should be closed out by the thirtieth of next month."

"Yes, O.K.," said Jesse. Quite a lot of money, and money was always nice to have, but the old man really shouldn't have done that. And then Jean looked in the door and said the Lannings were here, and Jesse didn't know what to say to them.

"You can see there isn't much we can do, until Mrs. Johnson shows up. I'm sorry I haven't been of more help."

"But she might be anywhere!" said Susan Lanning. "What you have found out—leaving her apartment, maybe gone off with this man—we don't know she'll ever come back here, or what's happening to Josie—" She looked wild.

"I must say, it doesn't seem very likely, if she's taken off with this Pierce, that they'd want Josie along. What do you think, Mr. Falkenstein?"

Jesse didn't know what to think. He dug his pen into the blotter. "Can you tell me," he asked abruptly, "exactly what she said—when she called you, when she came after Josie?"

Lanning said grimly, "I can. It was the—the baldness of it hit us both. She said maybe we thought she'd forgot all about us but she hadn't, and now she could take the baby off our hands, she'd be by next day to get her. She didn't give me a chance to talk back—it was all business, short and sweet. And that morning when she came—"

"Excuse me, should have asked before. In a car?"

"Why, yes. If it's any use, a Ford Galaxie, an old white four-door. She looked"—Lanning passed a hand across his balding brow—"so much older than we remembered her. She was such a pretty girl, she's still pretty, but—harder. Older. She just looked at Josie and said, excuse me, Jesus, is that her? And she hadn't thought she'd be so big. And then she—"

"Trying to make up to her," said Mrs. Lanning fiercely. "Josie didn't understand. And she didn't give us a chance—it was as if she just brushed us off—all Josie's things, I'd just packed a few things in an old suitcase of mine, a couple of good dresses, not even a change of shoes, I expected Nonie'd help me get the rest together, or— Just starting to take her away like that, and I said what about all her clothes, her toys, her books, we could bring them—she hadn't given us an address, if she'd tell us where— And she said she'd tell us where to send it all, but she didn't. She hasn't. And Fred actually hanging onto her, until she gave him that phone number. Mr. Falkenstein, it's two weeks on Sunday, and not a word, and now all this you've been telling us— Do you mean we just have to *wait*? Some more?"

"For what?" said Lanning reasonably. "What you've said, it doesn't seem that she's very close to what family she's got. She's been a drifter, no really close ties at all. Suppose she is away on this —this glamorous cruise with this Pierce fellow. And Josie—though that wouldn't make much sense. When she does come back, if she comes back here and not somewhere else, who's going to know? It's obvious she didn't mean to contact us again."

"Which is also something to think about," said Jesse. "I can't answer that one, Mr. Lanning. It's conceivable that if she doesn't show up in a reasonable time, say at that club to collect her back salary, you may have to think about a private eye to try to locate Josie."

"Oh, my God. That kind of money—not that it'd be any object, but I haven't got it."

Susan Lanning leaned forward and stared at Jesse with reddened eyes. "Mr. Falkenstein, she didn't want Josie—in herself—she wasn't feeling remorseful or guilty or *interested* in Josie at all. *Why did she take her*? Why? And now you're saying we might never see Josie again—this woman taking her somewhere and God knows what's happening to her—she didn't *care* about Josie, it was—like Fred says —like a dog we'd boarded for her, she smiled and said things like we'd been nice to do it, thanks, she was sorry it had been so long, but it was just talk. And now you're telling us there isn't even any way to find out where Josie is?"

Jesse put the pen down before he ruined it. "You know as much as I do. She's been a drifter, yes. A private eye might find her now, or not. But I'll say this. She seems to have stuck to this area, except for that one hiatus in Vegas. And she's never been so flush with money that she's apt to leave that back pay uncollected. She keeps in touch, if sporadically, with her sister Mrs. Lefkowitz and this girl friend

Rena Sawyer. I think the chances are good that she'll come back here, and one of them will let me know."

"And then what?" asked Lanning.

"And then we approach her and ask if she's still interested in keeping Josie. Believe in all the highfalutin ethics myself," said Jesse dryly, "but there are ways and means. If I throw out a hint that we might charge her with being an unfit parent, could be she'd be ready and willing to forget the whole thing. Could even be we'd get her to agree to an adoption."

Mrs. Lanning relaxed. "You think she'll come back after that money?"

"We can't even be sure she's gone," Jesse pointed out. "That's just inference. She could have moved a mile away from her old apartment, got another job. But I don't think so. It's probable she's with Pierce, and that she'll turn up in time. I know it isn't easy for you, but—"

"So we wait." Lanning got up. "Well, thanks. We'll just have to do some praying on it, then."

Damn it, thought Jesse as they went out, he was about ready to consult one of the psychics about this damned nebulous thing: see what clairvoyance could come up with about Nonie. There was no shape to it: there wasn't anything to get hold of. As a lawyer he liked nice solid facts that could be brought out and studied, and there were all too few here. One fact he was clinging to was that three eighty-five Harry owed Nonie for two weeks' worth of topless dancing. Wherever the girl went, wherever and whyever she'd taken Josie, she'd be back to collect that.

And he still thought Christine Lefkowitz knew something she hadn't told. Maybe not much, but something.

Jimmy looked in and said Mr. Dakin was here, and Jesse got up automatically.

As Clock had told Jesse, he didn't think anybody would ever get charged with McAllister's death: the evidence was too slim. But they had to go through the motions of working it, until that was obvious and it got tossed into Pending. Petrovsky went out to talk to some

more of the happy gamblers. Clock read the night-watch reports: the
A.P.B.s hadn't turned up either of the possible child molesters yet,
and there had been another heist job at a liquor store, two more burglaries and an attempted homicide.

On his way out he passed Detectives Guttierez and Emlyn in the
parking lot. "I don't know why we agitated to get the central air conditioning," said Emlyn disgustedly. "We don't get to stay in it
fifteen minutes of any shift." And there was more truth than poetry
in that.

Clock went out to Berendo Street to talk to Howard Gebhart's
neighbors. If Gebhart should have an alibi of sorts, that would make
it tidier: forget him.

Gebhart owned a modest house in that solid middle-class neighborhood in Hollywood, a rather ugly stucco box of a house on a
standard fifty-foot lot, with similar houses on each side. It was a
shame to set neighbors gossiping, but it couldn't be helped; Clock
brought out his badge and asked his questions economically. From a
Mrs. Hansen on one side he got a flood of vituperation. "It's no wonder crime's up all over if the cops spend their time going around poking their noses at honest respectable citizens, I never heard of such a
thing, asking about Howard Gebhart, lived here thirty years and a
finer man don't exist, what you're up to asking about Howard— And
how would I remember all that time ago, last Saturday night? I
don't remember, I don't take notice of neighbors coming and going
way some people do. This weather, we got the one room conditioner
in the den and that's where we'd be, with the windows shut naturally, and that's on the other side of the house, I couldn't say at all
and why you're wasting your time asking questions about a decent
citizen—" From Mrs. Whitlake on the other side he got indifference.
"I don't know, I'm sure. We just moved here last month, it's not the
class of place I'm used to and we don't know any of the neighbors."

Exercise in futility, thought Clock. Unless Pete turned up a hotter
lead, which he didn't expect, they'd do better to put this in Pending
right now and forget about it. There was enough else on hand.

At the precinct house, Mantella had some news. The victim of the
heist last night, a clerk at the liquor store, had been looking at mug
shots and positively identified X: George Lopez, just off parole, pedi-

gree of armed robbery, rape, assault. They were just about to put out the A.P.B. Something cleared out of the way, at least.

Petrovsky didn't show up until after lunch, when he said he'd talked to all the rest of that more or less regular bunch who'd sat in with McAllister, and he didn't think any of them had suspected more than a run of luck; by now, alerted by Bryant and Morrison, they were denouncing McAllister as a dirty crook, but there wasn't anything in it. Gebhart was the likeliest suspect and they'd never pin it on him, and McAllister was a small loss. "I'd like," said Petrovsky, "to sit here peacefully and type the report, Andrew. Do you think I'll get the chance?"

"No bets," said Clock. The phone rang on his desk and he picked it up.

"You've got a new homicide," said the desk sergeant. "The black-and-white just called in. They got sent to a family dispute over on Delongpre and by the time they got there the wife was stiff. Shot. They want detectives."

"Naturally," said Clock. Nobody else was in. "What's the address? O.K. Sorry, Pete, you don't get to stay in air conditioning. We're going out again."

Petrovsky got up with a groan. "They just announced another smog alert."

"Which is not irrelevant," said Clock. "The rate always goes up in a heat wave."

⊚⊚⊚

Jesse finally got down to clearing up some paper work after lunch, but his heart wasn't in it. The Lannings were still there at the back of his mind, and what the hell else could he have said to them? What the hell else was there to do? Legally, not a leg to stand on. The hell of it was, he thought to himself, that if Nonie had been available to get at, he felt morally sure that he—and/or the Lannings —could have argued her around into letting go of Josie. It was very possible that she was already regretting having taken Josie. And what would that mean to Josie?

At the worst, more gross neglect, he decided. But how the Lannings would be feeling— He realized at that point that he'd stopped proofreading the page before him five minutes ago and was staring at the portrait of Sir Thomas More wondering absently about getting in touch with ships at sea. Unofficially. What Pierce or Nonie did wasn't any of his business, or the Lannings; they had a right to privacy like everybody else. He couldn't cable the purser and ask.

The office door opened diffidently. "Have you got half an hour?"

"You'll probably want more," said Jesse, but he looked up with some relief. DeWitt came in and sat down; he was looking more serious than usual.

"I've got something here I want you to listen to, Jesse. I don't know what it's worth or what it might mean to you, but I thought—" DeWitt was silent and then asked, "The baby all right?"

"Flourishing," said Jesse, taken aback.

"Good." DeWitt opened the inevitable brief case but didn't at once lift the flap. "This is something a bit surprising. I'll give you some background in a minute, but after I'd heard it I thought it sounded —authentic enough—that you'd better have it immediately. I've got no idea what it might mean, which is just as well if it is authentic." He took a tape recorder out of the brief case.

Jesse looked at it with distaste. "Not one of your wild tapes, William."

"No." Diverted for the moment, DeWitt looked at the cassette player fondly. "What gadgets we have to play with these days—and how helpful. Shortcuts. So much more exact. When I think what a boon a simple tape recorder would have been to those old boys, counting raps on a Ouija board or taking notes in the dark at a trance sitting— These things save a lot of time, we always keep a tape running during sittings, to have an exact record."

"So what have you got there?"

"Something possibly for you," said DeWitt. "I don't know. This is part of a session with Wanda Moreno, late this morning. The sitting was for Jane Kerr, one of a continuing series. Proxy sitting, Miss Duffy representing Miss Kerr. We've had some very good evidential material in this series, the contactee being Miss Kerr's mother, who died last year. Nothing startling, the usual thing. Past incidences unknown to the medium or proxy sitter, names and so on. Of course Wanda is scarcely another Mrs. Osborne Leonard. God, if we had anything like some of those mediums today— She's a good clairvoyant, developing mediumship, not a powerful medium yet—possibly never. She doesn't aspire to direct voice, of course. There've been one or two suggestive hints just lately that she's coming under a definite control, which she hasn't had up to now—that'd be another step ahead. She doesn't often get into deep trance, sometimes not at all. But when she is in trance, the clairvoyance is stronger, and she's made some very good hits."

"Do I get to hear the tape?"

"In a minute. I want you to have the background. This was a sitting for Miss Kerr, and naturally what we were hoping to get was more communication from the mother. The Kerrs' background, of course, is totally unknown to the medium. The mother was a language teacher, French and Latin, her husband's name is Graham—he's still living—she had a daughter, Jane, and two sons, John and James. She died very suddenly in a plane accident at fifty-five. One of the sons is a physician, the other an artist. There have been clear references to all these points in other sessions, the inference being that she's interested in affording us clear evidence."

"All right, I've got that."

"I ran this part off for you on a new tape. Not the whole record, but I began it while some of the Kerr stuff was coming through so you could judge how the other bit broke in. Wanda was in a light trance, blood pressure and pulse normal. You'll notice, incidentally, that there's another hint here at a control trying to take possession."

"And you're going by the book, not giving me a hint what to expect."

"All right, here you are." DeWitt fiddled with the volume, turned the recorder around to face Jesse and pushed the PLAY button.

The tape lead ran around for ten seconds and the sound came on in the middle of a word. The voice was feminine, light and pleasant, sounding quite normal except for a slight breathiness. "—illing to co-operate, she is saying. She is pleased that G— G— someone called G— Gray is interested in this experiment. She is saying now— I don't understand this—non mort, she says. There is no—a word there I don't understand, wait, she is trying—there is no estimation, estimating how important this could be to the world. I can't see this person clearly now. It's as if she's going away into a mist, but just before she showed me a picture, a picture made of light, it's just a great big circle of light, and I think she meant something like coming full circle. *Oh!*" The voice conveyed a convulsive physical start. "There's someone else now, somebody quite different. It's a man. I can't see him, there's someone helping him, someone much stronger, because it is something—urgent, important, he says. The other one. He's trying very hard to get this through, if only I could see better, I must try to help—try to help them. Ur-gent, someone says. Try, try, try." The tape wound for a few breaths, emptily whirring, and then the voice broke in again on a deeper tone and suddenly louder. "Tell Jessie—tell Jessie—there is danger to the child, must find, tell Jessie! They're gone, I can't hear any more, and the other one is coming back, she says she had to let that one come because the power changed over. She's back."

DeWitt flicked the recorder off. He didn't say anything, watching Jesse. After a moment Jesse sat up and lit a cigarette. "My unfortunate name," he said. "I take it you don't number a Jessie, female, among your regular sitters or communicators."

"No, and of course it's pronounced the same for either sex. Does that mean anything to you? Don't tell me what, if anything. It's Greek to me. But could it refer to anything relating to you?"

"Rather surprising thing, it just could, William," said Jesse softly. "But it's so easy to read things in, isn't it? Even granting that's a valid communication from beyond, could be a warning from Grandpa to Jessie Smith to mind the baby."

"That's right," said DeWitt. "And all sorts of things come in. When I heard the name, maybe I skipped over a conclusion or two."

"Or maybe not," said Jesse. He was staring out the window.

DeWitt let out a sigh. "You've told me what I wanted to know. You think it could be."

"Reservations," said Jesse.

"So much of it is always borderline. Without a really strong medium—" DeWitt took off his glasses and began to polish them. "But that's why I gave you the background—we've had very valid evidence through Wanda, when she's at her highest level she's good, possibly as good as we can hope for these days. I don't want to know what that might mean to you. Write it out, date it, sign it with a witness, seal it up and give it to me for the files. In case it turns out to be important." He started to put the tape recorder into his brief case.

"All right," said Jesse. "And I'll keep that tape awhile, William."

DeWitt handed it over. He said, "You know we're not playing games here. The evidence is good evidence, but you have to study a good deal of it before you realize that. And any day—as an honest scientist, I like to think—I'd rather deal with one like you, who looks at it from every side before saying yes or no, than the true believer like Golding, say, who says yes to everything that shows up. You've had another thought about it?"

"Oh, yes," sighed Jesse. "I haven't got many people on the other side who might be urgently wanting to communicate. But there seem to be a good many disinterested well-wishers over there, pleased to help where they can."

"I suppose that means something to you," said DeWitt.

Jesse sat there at the big new desk for a while, staring absently at the tape on the blotter. What little they did know about it, it wasn't very easy for somebody over there to get back with a coherent message. Even when they wanted to. Urgently.

He picked up the page he'd been proofreading again, but didn't focus on it. He was uneasy, for no logical reason at all.

He remembered suddenly, the random thought, how he'd happened to meet old Edgar. That homicide, and the frame on Harry Nielsen, and the little girl who'd seen the killer saying he looked like Santa Claus. Old Edgar, retired from the department store he owned, playing Santa Claus for the kids.

He got up and put the tape in his pocket. He went out and said to the Gordons, "See you on Monday." He didn't notice the brow-raising looks they gave each other. Downstairs, he got into the Dodge and drove up Highland to Fountain, swung over to the residential side street Kingsley.

He could have guessed the kind of house the Lannings would have: an old California bungalow painted white with green trim. The front lawn was looking a little brown, in the heat wave; they'd be careful about the water bill, and Lanning wouldn't have been feeling like yard work. The deep front porch would shade the front rooms, but there was a room air conditioner installed in the left front window. A middle-aged Chrysler was parked in the drive. As Jesse went up the front walk a dog barked sharply inside.

Lanning opened the door. "Mr. Falkenstein—"

"Nothing new," said Jesse. He went into the kind of room he expected: comfortable. Rather shabby old furniture, slipcovered, a nice oak dining set at one end of the long room. Plain beige carpet, a seascape on the wall over the couch. "I just got to thinking. Would you like me to spend a little money, try to find out definitely whether Nonie's with Pierce and Josie with her?"

"C-could you?" asked Mrs. Lanning.

"Don't know. Look into it. See if the ship line would be co-operative, contact the purser on that liner. It'd probably involve a few long-distance calls, I suppose the company's based in New York or Miami."

The Lannings looked at each other. "I think we'd like you to try," said Lanning slowly. "It would be something definite, at least."

"I thought so. I'd like to know something definite too," said Jesse. "I'll get on it. Don't know what I could do tomorrow—if there'd be an office open anywhere on Saturday. I'll find out, let you know."

They nodded at him quietly.

◎◎◎

Clock and Petrovsky booked the husband in by three o'clock. It hadn't been anything to work because the uniformed men had practically witnessed the shooting. And if the thankless job of being a cop had its lighter moments, that was one of them. The husband was Leo O'Brien, a big fat red-headed man in his forties, and he'd just sat and scowled at them there in the tiny-roomed, crowded apartment in an old four-family place on the tired narrow old street in the middle of Hollywood. There wasn't even an electric fan, and he was perspiring profusely. The body was on the floor, a slim dark woman with a lovely dark tan; she was wearing shorts and a halter-necked bra.

They hadn't even had to question him. The neighbors had heard them arguing and called the cops, and the uniformed men had just parked in front when they heard the shots.

"I had," said O'Brien, breathing heavily, "just had it. But good.

Enough. The last time. What I did to please that woman. Shorten my life by ten years, I swear. She was born here. So was I, but I was bright enough to get out. I had a good job up the coast, in Santa Cruz. Beautiful up there, beautiful, the ocean, the sea breezes, cold nights even in summer, lots of rain—I felt good up there. I even like the fog."

"Yes, Mr. O'Brien?" Clock had taken the gun from one of the Traffic men, an Old Colt .38.

"She can't stand it away from her family and friends, it's too cold, she can't stand it, she keeps at me till I quit and we come back here. That's enough!" said O'Brien violently. "It is damn well enough to do for her, I'm back in this goddamn foretaste of hell, just to please her. Without her throwing it in my face, by God. With it's a hundred and four today and more smog, I'm sitting here sweating like a pig, she comes waltzing in and she says it to me again. A thousand times she said it. And that last time did it. That really did it."

"What did she say?" asked Petrovsky.

"She says, oh, I just love this nice hot weather, and that *did* it!" said O'Brien. He looked at them broodingly and wiped sweat off his face. "At least I'll never hear her say that again."

Clock was thinking about the O'Briens as they drove back to the office; Fran did have a point there, as long as they were going in debt for the house— Tomorrow was his day off, and he thought they could get some estimates on the central air conditioning at least.

"Anything new down?" he asked the desk sergeant.

"Another molester—six-year-old girl off a park playground. Mantella's out on it."

"Damnation," said Clock. "I wonder if it's the same one. I'd like to pick up that bastard."

⊚⊚⊚

"I don't know what to think about it," said Nell. "I don't know what to say. It's—out of my depth, Jesse. I know, you've shoved some of the books at me, and there's a lot can't be explained away. It isn't all silly wishful thinking. But about this—when it's close to home—maybe nobody can judge fairly."

"One of the many difficulties," said Jesse. He was wandering around the front room with a drink in his hand; Athelstane watched him mournfully.

"If I did think—" said Nell, and stopped, and went on, "we can't imagine how, but—over there, some of them—seem to see a little way ahead. Warnings— If I did think that, I'd be worried about the baby. First. And I'm not, especially."

"Dimensions of time," said Jesse. "Damn it. Damn it, Nell. It wasn't all that damned tape did it. Dangerfield, this morning, and damn, I forgot to go and sign his red tape. Got me thinking about the old boy. Damn it, Nell, it's a trite thing to say—we take people for granted. Just here. And then not. He was lonely and bored since he'd retired, and that damn family of his—no reason to say that, nice people, but conventional, didn't appreciate him because he wasn't. Tiresome interfering old man, sitting on him because he liked a drink—why the hell shouldn't he, not much else left to him. They had their own interests. But he always liked people—all kinds of people—interested in them. What makes them tick. He was sharp as they come, and I thought it gave him something to think about, little interest in life—drop into the office, hear about the latest case. Andrew too. Damn it, he'd be so pleased if I said, come on in, sit down. Damn it, he was so happy when Fran and Andrew got engaged—"

"Jesse—"

"Damn it to hell, I wish he hadn't made that will. No, I don't— the money's always very nice, but— Oh, hell," said Jesse, "I wish we'd paid more attention, is all. Done more. Times he came by and I was busy. Times we could have called him, come over to dinner."

"You always wish that when somebody's gone," said Nell. "You don't need the will to know he thought a lot of you. Of us."

After a long pause Jesse said, "He always tried to help, you know. When I was stuck over something. He liked helping people. And he liked children."

"I really don't know," said Nell, "why you're using the past tense. Habit. If we're mentioning evidence, it seems to say that people don't change much all of a sudden, just being gone from here."

"That's so," said Jesse with a sharp sigh. He finished the drink, went into the den and Nell heard him switch on the phonograph. Knowing the symptoms, she went to shut the door to the nursery.

Some experts agreed that exposure to the fine arts was beneficial even to very young infants, but all Nell needed was another sleepless night, and she didn't really suppose that David Andrew would be enthralled by Bach.

The "Toccata and Fugue in D Minor" swelled from the den and she went thoughtfully out to the kitchen to do the dinner dishes, followed by the silent padding shadow of Athelstane.

With a policewoman standing by, the detectives talked as well as they could to the six-year-old. She hadn't been hurt, had remembered all mama and daddy said about strange men and told the crossing guard at the playground about him. The playground was off Adams Boulevard, about a mile from where the man had approached Edna Moorhead.

"He said his name was Don," the six-year-old told Mantella. She had shied away from Clock's unhandsome craggy face and he retired to the background. "He had glasses on. He said he had a kitten in his car and would I like to see it."

It wasn't much use to ask her about height, weight, age. They'd already talked to the crossing guard and he hadn't noticed a thing. It was a big playground, a lot of traffic going by.

The parents arrived, the father savage, the mother tearful, and took her away. "Don," said Clock. "Does that ring any bells? The mug shots Mrs. Moorhead picked out—" He scrabbled in his desk for the Xeroxed pedigree sheets from R. and I. "Well, that could spell it out," and he handed one to Mantella. "William Donald Lightner. He's been known to use his middle name before. Maybe pins it down a little tighter. And if it's him, he's also the boy on that rape—that's where we got the best description."

"These kooky bastards," said Mantella. "D.M.V. gave us a plate number. Let's hope the A.P.B. brings him in."

Josie sat on the saggy old couch clutching the book to her thin chest. She wasn't reading it, she didn't want to read it, but in a queer way it felt good to be touching it, a familiar world, a world she loved, where Mr. Toad and Water Rat and Mole lived and had fun. It was a world like home, and connected with home, a long long way off.

Things changed fast here, where things never changed at home. She tried to think back just to the other day, the day Denny had taken her out, and she'd thought he was stupid about the library card. The other day in the playground. She'd thought, nice, friendly. Not now. Not since he and Mama had the fight.

A lot of loud talk and swear words, they were both awful mad and yelling, and then they'd shut her in here, the door locked, she remembered just that one minute clear—how the hell did I know she'd be a half-grown kid could talk plain—and then the door slammed and Denny yelling something else. And noises, things falling. And when the door got opened, Mama had a big dark mark on her face and her mouth had blood on it.

Denny had taken her out to the playground, that was the day before, or sometime, and swung her on the swings and bought her an ice-cream cone, but after the fight she'd got to be scared of Denny too.

It was starting to get dark. Drearily, Josie looked at her clean dresses hanging up on the closet door. It was a while before the fight she'd finally asked, and Mama had looked and said, "Oh, hell, I never thought about—damn, that woman said, but—" And, "Damn, I suppose somebody'll have to see you sometime," and she'd taken Josie's clothes and after a while brought them back all clean. The dresses were what was called wash-wear, didn't have to be ironed, and it was nice to have them clean again, and clean underclothes.

But she didn't feel so much of anything about Mama as about Denny, now. A hollow feeling inside, it was. She'd thought nice, and then he was all red in the face and yelling and bunching his fists up and swearing. She'd never watched TV much, Mother Sue didn't let her, but the first days here, nothing to do, and Denny had it on mostly, and she'd watched it with him. It made time pass, whatever was on, and because she'd never seen it much it was kind of interesting, people talking, playing games, sometimes cartoons, fast-talking people shouting at you, pictures of cars, pretty girls, people shooting and kissing and laughing. But after the fight and Denny yelling,

Josie couldn't watch TV any more, in there with him. He'd be there too close, sitting in front of it.

He was bigger than Daddy Fred, and awful strong. Mama had yelled back at him, but she was scared of him. Josie saw.

She didn't know why she had to be here. They didn't want her, they were just keeping her. Once, a long while ago, she'd thought about just going home—it had seemed easy in her mind, the taxi cab, you called and it came and took you home, and Daddy Fred would pay, even seven dollars—she didn't know where to tell it to come, but if she could get out of the apartment, away, she could find out, names on streets. Then, planning it out, and she'd thought despairingly, a dime. It cost a dime to phone anywhere, when you weren't at home.

At home.

And he was there, where there was a phone here. Except, now, the times they were both gone. With the apartment door locked.

It was dark now and the EATS sign flashed on and off.

All of a sudden Josie began to get the choking feeling. She hadn't had that in a long while, and it was nightmare and panic and the dark coming down. And all in a flash she thought, she's forgot to say her prayers all the while she'd been here—all the while away from home—that was why, God didn't like it, her forgetting her prayers. She sat bolt upright on the couch and dropped the book and began to say the words, but they wouldn't come out right after the first part, Our Father who art in heaven— It got all mixed up, she couldn't remember, that was terrible, and the panic struck her and the choking feeling got worse—

Once when she was just little, it was so bad Mother Sue called the firemen, and something over her face—

EATS, said the sign, EATS EATS. Josie gasped for breath and tried desperately to remember— Our Father who art in heaven—

SEVEN

On Saturday morning, looking for shortcuts and expecting none, Jesse tried that travel agency and surprisingly talked to Miss Reising. "Well, so somebody works on Saturday. I wonder if you can tell me, does somebody else?"

She was smiling, by her tone. "Any way I can help you, Mr. Falkenstein." And to his question, "Well, it's a big line, they have offices here. The cruise liners are just the cream at the top, I suppose, they've got freighters going all over, Creston Cruises is just one of the names, it's really Gorbal and Cross Freight Line."

"Oh," said Jesse.

"I've got an address somewhere," and she gave him one on Long Beach Boulevard. He tried the number, and the phone whirred emptily at the other end. Saturday. Saying this and that, Jesse consulted the Yellow Pages himself, and found an additional address given— Pier D, East Basin, Long Beach Harbor. That sounded like the workaday address where there might be people who actually had something to do with the ships.

It was just as hot today, and it wouldn't be any cooler down there; that side of the bay was always twenty degrees hotter than Santa Monica. Jesse, annoyed by his overlarge conscience, got onto the Harbor freeway and drove down to Long Beach. He had to leave the car in a lot along the harbor front and plod up and down great expanses of docks past a variety of ships; he finally found a tall cavern of a dockside warehouse labeled Gorbal and Cross in smudged, weathered paint. There was a crew of men at work on stacks of wooden packing cases, a rusty-looking huge freighter tied up at the nearest slip. Jesse approached the man apparently in charge of the crew, a burly individual checking a fistful of yellow manifest lists.

"Anybody in authority?" he repeated, staring at Jesse. "You mean like somebody from the front office? The board chairmen don't load the cargo, mister. Mr. Galen's inside if he's any good to you." Jesse followed the jerked finger indicating direction and eventually found a small tidy office beyond more towering stacks of packing crates, and, by the neat sign on the door, MR. PETER J. GALEN, SUPERINTEND-ENT.

Jesse considered Galen, the other man looking up at him inquiringly from paper work, a little impatient. Galen was about forty, with friendly eyes and a firm mouth. There was a framed picture on his desk of a nice-looking dark-haired woman and three children, aged about twelve on down to three, two boys and a girl.

"I've got a queer little problem, Mr. Galen," he said. "Don't know if you can help me." He gave him a card.

"Don't often see a lawyer in here," said Galen. He swept some loose-leaf folders off the only other chair. "Sit down. What's your problem?"

Taking the long chance, Jesse outlined the story for him concisely. "Now, you can see that we'd all like to know something definite. That liner isn't due back in Miami until two weeks from Monday. I've got no official status to send out any inquiries, there's such a thing as right to privacy. But if there's any way at all to find out, unofficially, if it is Mrs. Johnson with Pierce on that cruise, and if the child's with them, I'd like to know. Is there?"

Galen had listened interestedly, fiddling with his pen, a cigarette. He laid the pen down and lit a new cigarette with an old-fashioned kitchen match from a box on the desk. "That's a hell of a thing," he said thoughtfully. "Little girl that age, snatched away from the only home she's known. I've got one of my own. Ordinarily, Mr. Falkenstein, there are pretty strict regulations about ship-to-shore communication. Aside from private cablegrams, and as you say that's no use to you. No reason these people should answer you at all. And any messages to the ship, officially, go through the company or, of course, the radio-weather stations. But two weeks—" He picked up the pen again. "I shouldn't even consider it, but it might be we could do something unofficial."

"Like what?"

"I'm in touch with all the line's offices, of course, on a regular basis. I know a fellow in the Miami office who's in our communications bureau there, one of the men who'll be sending out the normal messages, ship-to-shore, to the various captains and pursers in that territory. I can't guarantee anything, but if I give him a ring and ask, it could be if he has a legitimate occasion to contact the *Princess Pat* in the next few days, he could slip in a query to the purser."

"I'd be very much obliged."

Galen shrugged. "It's just a chance. I won't even ask you to pay for the call, it's a company phone. It's irregular, but what the hell. This woman would probably be traveling as that fellow's wife, I suppose. And these liners carry four, five hundred passengers, it's not likely the purser would have heard her first name. Nonie, you said. But he'd know about any children on board, and especially if there was some last-minute arrangement. I'll try to get hold of Bill today— the time difference, he'll be in the office till three here—and see what he says."

"I'd appreciate it," said Jesse.

"I'll let you know. Even if Bill has some reason to contact the ship, it might not be right away."

"Just let me know if you get anything—that's my home phone. Thanks, Mr. Galen—I can see you're going out on a limb, I appreciate it."

"I don't guarantee a thing," said Galen, smiling slightly.

◎◎◎

Wilcox Street was two plainclothesmen short on Saturday, Clock and Mantella off. Petrovsky was the only one in, reading a lab report on the latest burglary, at two-thirty, when surprisingly the McAllister case took on a little new life. The desk sergeant called up to say that a new witness had just come in, he was sending him up.

Curiously, Petrovsky put down the report to welcome the witness. When he limped in a minute later, Petrovsky regarded him disappointedly, but that was premature. He was at least eighty, tall and thin and stooped, and he leaned on a cane; he had a lined, jowly face like an elderly bloodhound, and thin white hair carefully plastered over a pink scalp. "You the detective?" he demanded a little breathlessly.

"That's right, sir. Detective Petrovsky. Sit down. What can I do for you?"

"Other way round. My name's Shaughnessy, Alonzo J. Haven't had to climb stairs in a while, let me get my breath." He lowered himself into the chair with a relieved sigh, and went on, "That's some better. Come to the point right away, I live at the Borland Hotel on Highland. Never heard a thing about that murder till today. But there's nothing surprising about that because I don't go out hardly at all."

"Oh," said Petrovsky. "Did you know Roger McAllister, Mr. Shaughnessy?"

"Never laid eyes on him. Gather he used his place there for sleeping and that's about all. I'm there most of the time, since I retired. Used to have a little short-order sandwich stand at the corner of La Brea and Olympic—over thirty years I ran it, a good living and I liked meeting all the different people—but the arthritis caught up to me about ten years ago and I had to give it up. With the Social Security and what I'd saved up, I get along all right, got a nice single apartment there, and I've always been one for reading, I like crossword puzzles too, I keep occupied. Happy as a clam all week there, maybe go out once or twice to the drugstore down the street, after ice cream or something, maybe not. And on Saturdays my daughter Helen comes up from Santa Monica and takes me grocery shopping and the library. So it wasn't till today I heard about the murder."

"I see," said Petrovsky.

"And I don't know that what I got to say'd be of any help to you, but being a responsible citizen I figured I'd better come in and tell you. Helen wanted to come in with me, but I said 'twasn't needful, look as if I needed a nursemaid. I still got all my buttons, and I know what I saw. My eyes are as good as they ever were, it's only my knees don't work right any more."

"So what did you see?" asked Petrovsky, smiling.

"I asked the desk clerk some more about it when we got back from the library, and he said the detectives reckoned that fellow got killed last Saturday night. It was then I recollected this and thought I better come in. Now first I better tell you, my place's on the top floor, and they let me use the freight elevator, come and go, which is handy. Helen thought I'd get better air on the top floor. I got a fan, but it don't do much more than stir the air up, and I don't need to tell you it's been almighty hot. Now, dang it, I didn't tell you, furthermore, my place is on the side toward that parking lot, that's right next the hotel—where you found the man."

"Oh," said Petrovsky.

"And last Saturday night I couldn't get to sleep. Tossed and turned awhile, got up and put on the light and tried to read, but somehow didn't feel like it for once. It'd be somewhere between 1 and 2 A.M. I got up and looked out of the window."

"Any reason?" asked Petrovsky.

"Get a breath of air. Hardly any traffic that time o' night, but lights all still on, and lights in that parking lot. And just as I was looking out, there was a car drove into the lot. No, I couldn't see what kind, up that high, but it wasn't a big car and it was gray on top. It parked, right up at the end of the lot next the alley, and then before anybody got out of it, a fellow come walking up to it, and kind of bent down and said something to whoever was in the gray car, and got in it. He come out of another car parked there—like he'd been waiting for the other fellow, see."

"You couldn't hear what he said."

"A-course not, way up there. I went on standing there, it was starting to get some cooler then, and a-course I wasn't paying much attention to that car down there. But about, oh, maybe six, eight minutes later I heard a car door slam, and looked, and somebody got out of that gray car and went back to the other one and drove off. You understand, I didn't have no reason to think anything was wrong, it was just something I noticed."

"From the fourth floor," said Petrovsky thoughtfully. "I don't suppose you could say anything about the other man, or the car?"

"Bein' an honest man, I'd have to say not much. Even if I'd been any closer, why should I take any notice? No reason. I was just having a mouthful of air at the window. But like I say, that lot's lighted at night, and he didn't go out onto Highland, he backed around and drove out the alley, and I saw the car just a second there when it turned, and it was light blue. I got no idea what kind but it was bigger than the other one."

"Well, well," said Petrovsky to himself. It was still nothing of a case, legally; and a jury probably wouldn't think much of

Shaughnessy. But that was interesting. Gebhart drove a light blue Mercury sedan.

"I just thought I better come and tell you."

"We appreciate it, Mr. Shaughnessy. If we want a formal statement, we'll let you know. Would you like a ride home, sir?"

"Oh, Helen's waiting for me, thanks. Just hope it helps you some. Way these criminals are all over the place these days, got to help out the cops."

In a way Petrovsky was sorry he'd come in. The McAllister thing had been dying a natural death, and would probably have got stashed in Pending by tomorrow. This wasn't going to make any difference, but just to be thorough, having this, Clock would probably want to haul Gebhart in and question him again. Which would be a waste of time, but it had better be done.

◎◎◎

Clock had an expensive day off. When he and Fran got home at five o'clock, he had signed away upwards of five thousand bucks: a city employee was considered a good risk. The salesman had definitely promised that a crew would be out next Wednesday, well, no later than Thursday, to start installing the central air conditioning.

Clock stopped in front of the gate and Fran got out to open it and scoop up Sally. Sally, who like most Pekes was a holy terror and very brainy, and had once nearly murdered a burglar, licked Fran's chin. Clock drove through, Fran shut the gate and they all went in.

"I'll just feed her while you mix drinks. There's steaks for later on. Thank heaven they can come next week, I had visions of them saying not until December."

Relaxing, even in the stuffy house baked through by the sun, over a drink ten minutes later, Clock regarded her there opposite and thought, humbly, how unlikely it was that she had married him. Slim, smart, svelte Fran, who could have married anybody.

"You seem happy enough these days. Satisfied, nothing to do but be a housewife?" She'd had an important job editing a house fashion sheet.

"Darling, I'm loving it," said Fran. "That rat race of a job was boring me to death."

◎◎◎

Galen called Jesse on Sunday afternoon. "I got through to Bill, Mr. Falkenstein. He said he'd slip your query through if he has any reason to contact the *Princess Pat* in the next few days. I couldn't say when it might be, but I'll let you know if anything turns up."

Jesse thanked him again and debated whether to pass this on to the Lannings. It wasn't really anything, and might get their hopes up where it wasn't justified.

Nell was busy with the baby; Jesse wandered into the den and stood looking at that tape cassette lying on the desk. He didn't know at all what he thought about that tape. He started some Bach on the phonograph, toning down the volume, and stretched out on the couch. Presently, Nell wandered in and said, "I've finished that book," and began to look around the shelves for another. Jesse watched her from under half-closed lids for ten minutes, got up and looked and handed her *The Mystery of the Human Double*. She looked at it, put it back and walked out with *The ESP Reader*.

And damn it, he had to be in court all week—that damage suit. Conceivably it might even trail over into the following week.

◎◎◎

Sunday was just another day for cops. This one started out as Sunday usually did at a city precinct house, because Saturday night usually saw a little more action on the streets. The night watch had left reports on three heists, a knifing, a gang rumble and some wholesale vandalism to cars parked on the street along Sunset and Hollywood Boulevard. The A.P.B.'s were still out on Lopez, Lightner and Donahue. There were still two unidentified bodies found on the Hollywood beat, waiting in the morgue; one they hadn't seen an autopsy report on as yet.

Clock heard what Petrovsky had to say about Shaughnessy, and agreed. It was just worth questioning Gebhart again, but that was all. Unless Gebhart admitted killing McAllister, which was very unlikely, this didn't help to build a case against him. "It just makes me a little surer, Pete. I think it was Gebhart, but I doubt very much of it was a deliberate kill, and there's nothing solid to base a charge on." Clock sighed. "He'll probably be at home—no point in hauling him down here."

But before they got away from the office, calls started to come in from Traffic: a sniper on the Hollywood freeway, a pile-up, three known dead already. All the detectives in—Clock, Petrovsky and Guttierez—went out on that in a hurry, and it was a mess. The sniper had been somewhere up in the hills around the Hollywood Bowl, with a high-powered rifle, and he hadn't managed to shoot anybody but he'd brought death and mayhem down there. An old Caddy, its left front tire shot out, had gone out of control and rammed a car in the next lane: eventually there were four lanes piled up, two cars over the center divider, three corpses and five more injured. While the paramedics and the Traffic men sorted it out, the detectives and some more Traffic men spread out above the Bowl looking. They found several spent casings: the rifle looked like an Enfield. But it was hopeless, a lot of tall brush up there, plenty of cover, and after an hour they decided he was long gone, having had his little fun.

"I swear to almighty God," said Clock, wolfing down a hamburger —he and Petrovsky had stopped for an early lunch after all the exercise, "there's something gone wrong with people these days, Pete. The things that happen. God knows there's nothing new about murder and rape and theft, but it's the twisted minds, the kooks running around—" He chewed for a minute, swallowed and added, "You can understand a man like Gebhart—that's a straightforward thing. He was mad at McAllister for cheating him, and if he tackled him about it square and straight and ended up killing him, it was more or less an accident. But that crazy bastard back there getting his kicks firing a rifle at a crowded freeway—it makes you wonder about people."

Petrovsky yawned and agreed that it did. It was just as hot today, and the smog was the kind that got into your eyes. "You want to go see Gebhart?"

"Let's go back to the station and air conditioning for a while, catch up on the paper work. He won't run away," said Clock dourly.

They were still there, the only ones in, an hour later when the desk sergeant relayed a call from Traffic. There was a new body, he said.

And that, as Clock said later, was the sickest joke of the week, because it was a very old body indeed.

A party of riders from a stable up in Griffith Park had found the body: or rather the dog they had with them had sniffed it out, up the other side of Wattles Garden Park. Technically it was just inside Wilcox Street's territory. Clock and Petrovsky went up to have a look, calling up a morgue wagon to follow. There was a black-and-white marking the spot on the only access road below; they left the Pontiac and toiled up the steep brush-grown hill. On a trail above they could see six or seven horses, the blue uniforms of the Traffic men.

"This is adding insult to injury," said Petrovsky, "twice in one day."

"And if you ask me," panted Clock, achieving the crest of the hill, "that constitutes cruelty to dumb animals, taking them up in the hills on a day like this, out in the noon sun." The horses looked rather weary and disgruntled, standing around up there, their teenage riders were still excited and asking questions a mile a minute, and a scrappy little terrier was yelping, tied to one of the nearby trees.

"And I really do ask you," said Clock three minutes later, "what the hell we are supposed to do with that." He stood up, fumbling for a cigarette, wishing he hadn't had that hamburger. Or at least not with all the trimmings. Cops had to get used to bloody messes and corpses of all kinds, but some of them were worse than others. And some things you never quite did get used to.

It wasn't a pleasant corpse. It might, as one of the men from the morgue said, have been there two days or two months. It had been partly under some bushes; and this was a city park area, where the Parks and Recreation people had jurisdiction. It was all left in a natural state, but there were all the roadside pipes with arc sprinklers along here, to keep it green and wetted down against brush fires. The morgue attendants deduced that the corpse had lain just right to get wetted down by the sprinklers part of the time, and then baked in the sun; the results were devastating. You couldn't tell if it had been a man or woman, young or old, black or white, or have any guess at how long it had been a corpse.

"I wish the surgeons joy on this one," said Petrovsky. One of the teen-agers had got away from the Traffic men to take a look, and was being sick in the bushes.

"Oh, take it in," said Clock to the morgue attendants. "See what the doctors make of it. I don't think it'll make any work for us."

That time, to get back to something saner, they drove down to Berendo Street to talk to Gebhart. They told him how they'd read it, how they thought things had happened in that parking lot: him waiting for McAllister, accusing him. They told him they didn't think he'd meant to kill him.

"How about it, Mr. Gebhart? We'd all like to clear this up, get at the truth."

"Well, you got the right of it one way," said Gebhart. "I not only didn't mean to kill him, I didn't. I never went to see him that night —I was just going to leave him alone. Nothing like that happened and you can't prove it ever did."

Which was all too true, and as Clock said, it didn't matter a damn, really.

◎◎◎

Jesse stopped by Dangerfield's office on his way to the Civic Center on Monday morning and affixed his signature in the necessary places. He went on to spend a boring morning in court, over the preliminaries to that damage suit. He challenged one of the panel called for the jury and got into an argument, very politely conducted, with the bench. When the noon recess was called they didn't even have a jury, and he was feeling exasperated with the whole legal system.

One of the D.A.'s men had been sitting in as observer, and followed him out of the court. "You won't have any trouble with this as soon as it comes out we're prosecuting the defendant for fraud. Which is part of your legitimate evidence."

"You'll get a subpoena to testify," said Jesse gloomily, and sought a pay phone to call his office. There hadn't been any word from Galen, said Jean.

Court convened again at two and recessed at four in the middle of the first witness's testimony. Quite often Jesse agreed with the Gordons: what these judges did to earn their money— Old-fashioned bankers' hours you could say. There wasn't much he could do at the office in the hour remaining of the day, and for lack of anything else to do he dropped in at the Wilcox Street precinct, found Clock in and heard the story on McAllister.

"So that's that," said Clock. "Not another lead on it, no useful lab evidence, so we'll stash it in Pending. The body's already buried. Nobody seems to be missing him much, the poor bastard. Just a sordid little kill for money, and not much money at that."

"*In the death of a man there is no remedy,*" said Jesse. "Motives of human people don't matter so much, Andrew—it's who has them."

"And if we're quoting, there's another one that says money is the root of all evil."

"No, it doesn't," said Jesse querulously. "I wish to God people wouldn't quote unless they do it right. Same like taking things out of context, reviewing a book—and that one, various people get a lot of mileage out of, trying to prove the Bible's against capitalism. What it says is, the love of money is the root of all evil. Materialism. Which makes more sense, when you know anything about people."

"Well, it's a thing you won't have to worry about from now on," said Clock. "Sorry, Jesse, it just slipped out. I know—I miss the old reprobate too. I know you wish he hadn't left you that bundle."

"Who says I'm not as fond of money as the next man? It's not important unless you don't have it," said Jesse moodily.

"Well, I've just got rid of some of it," and Clock told him about the air conditioning. Jesse finished his latest cigarette, borrowed a phone and called his office. Nothing had been heard from Galen.

"I'd better go home," said Jesse, unhitching his lean frame from the corner of Clock's desk.

"How are you coming with your blond and the snatch, by the way?"

"I'm not. And going back to the last subject but one, as per Humpty-Dumpty," said Jesse, "I wish to hell and back I had the old man here, to ask him what he thinks about it. Maybe I'm missing something obvious—have a kind of uneasy feeling I am—but I can't put a finger on it. Same like with you and McAllister, no more leads to follow up. Nowhere to go. Nothing to do. And speaking of money, there's none in it, for me or anybody. Just some more heartbreak and misery for the Lannings, for Josie."

"It's the Lannings I feel sorry for," said Clock. "Kids can be pretty damn resilient—adjust to a lot. The Lannings have lost a hell of a lot more."

"I don't know," said Jesse. "I just don't know, Andrew. I'd better go home."

◎◎◎

The baby got them up at one o'clock. There wasn't anything wrong with him, said Nell crossly, except that he was, expectably, a night owl. And while she and Jesse were both night people who got progressively more brilliant up to midnight, a line had to be drawn somewhere and he'd have to learn to sleep at night. For one thing, she felt like a fool singing nursery rhymes in the middle of the night.

"Very unmaternal," said Jesse, squinting at his steadily yelling son. "I said we ought to try him on Bach or Haydn. If there's anything in genetics—"

"I don't know which might annoy the neighbors more," said Nell Athelstane, that conscientious dog, had come into the nursery with them, but he was looking sleepy too.

It was nearly three o'clock when the baby settled down and they went back to bed. Consequently, Jesse was not feeling even as bright as usual when he left for the office on Tuesday morning, half an hour late. As night people, he was never operating on all cylinders before noon anyway, and this morning he was still yawning as he rode up in the elevator. He had to be in court at ten; he'd have a look at the mail and just make the Civic Center in time.

But the Gordons greeted him with news. "The D.A.'s office has been calling like mad. The defendant in that suit, Henry Steele, shot himself last night and the suit's been called off. They want all your statements for it, and there's a man from the D.A.'s office coming anytime—"

"Well, I'll be damned," said Jesse. "Unexpected vacation, girls." He'd allowed at least five days for that court session, cleared the agenda to be free. "Now I expect we try to get a settlement from the estate, if any, and that'll be like pulling teeth. You'd better sort out the paper work for the D.A."

"We already have," said Jimmy.

The man from the D.A.'s office arrived and spent half an hour discussing that. "Of course the suicide's a tacit admittal of guilt, I don't expect your client will have much trouble getting some kind of settlement."

"Take no bets," said Jesse. After the D.A.'s man left, he sat there looking out the window and reflecting dismally that this had just given him more time to worry about Josie. When the door opened behind him he swiveled around reluctantly, half expecting to see De-Witt; and he didn't especially want to see DeWitt this morning.

It was only Jean. She said formally, "Will you see Mrs. Lefkowitz, Mr. Falkenstein?"

"Shoot her in," said Jesse casually. He stood up. He felt a little bolt of adrenaline slide through him. Glimmer of conscience, he'd said about Nonie. Oh, yes? Maybe a family trait. He remembered suddenly that Tuesday was her day off.

She came in slowly, looking around, looking at him and away. She had dressed up to come here, and she was a good-looking woman, smart in her plain navy sun dress, red sandals, red plastic costume jewelry, big red bag, her taffy-blond hair loose about her triangular face; she wore a good deal more makeup than when he'd seen her before.

"Sit down," he said easily. "What can I do for you?"

She took her time; she sat down deliberately, accepted a light for her cigarette, settled herself with slim legs crossed. She said finally, "I had to think this one out, Mr. Falkenstein. There was a lot to think about. Not for me, really anything to do with me, but Nonie. But the more I thought about it, even when I promised her I wouldn't tell, I could see maybe I'd better tell you. Because of—those people. So they won't—try to make any trouble."

"Is that so?" Jesse folded his hands across his lean middle and regarded her interestedly. "I had the feeling you knew something, Mrs. Lefkowitz."

"My God," she said, "I wish I'd started using my own name again, Lefkowitz, what a mouthful. Yeah. I kind of thought you did. I thought and thought about it, but finally I decided you better know.

On account of those people." She put out her cigarette, immediately lit another, flicked a nervous glance at him and then she leaned forward and it all came out in a rush.

"She came to see me on Friday night—that was two weeks ago last Friday—and she told me all about it. You're one that sees things, I guess I don't have to spell things out to you. I told you it had always been pretty hard going for all of us, about Mom—Martha doesn't count, she's got a husband she's satisfied with, stupid bum but he earns a living—but Nonie, she'd never had much. That bastard walking out, leaving her with a kid—taking what jobs she could get, she'd never made so much before, before she took the job at that club. When she told me about this, I knew just how she felt, see. You shouldn't go thinking it was like she was looking down her nose at us, Mom and me, it was just, a girl like Nonie don't get a chance like that once in a lifetime, and I know how she felt.

"She'd met this guy, she told me, a real wonderful guy. It was like Fate or something, she said. He wasn't like anybody she'd ever dated, I mean, the kind of guys she had a chance to meet, what were they?—ones who came to that club, ones like McAllister—nothings —ordinary guys, little jobs if they had any, no money, no nothing. What's the percentage, you get to feeling romantic and marry one like that? She was better off working that club and having her own money. But she met this guy, and it was the chance of a lifetime, see?

"She said, like Fate. How it happened. McAllister knew some people, a Ken something, had a beach cabin, and they were there one day, and she went down the beach alone and just ran into this guy there, they got talking and hit it off together right away. He was— she said—but something else—" Chris gestured impatiently, searching for words. "I don't mean she said it all starry-eyed, like that. She meant—he'd been to college, he talked kind of fancy, he was in the chips, like maybe a"—she looked around—"an office like this—you get what I mean. No, she didn't say anything about that, she was like being careful, but she knew, she just didn't say—I got the idea he was a doctor, lawyer, somebody like that.

"She never told him all about herself, that was it, she said. She could see what he'd think of the job at the club, she told him she

worked in a store. They dated a few times, him coming to her apartment to pick her up—and, see, McAllister found out, I told you he
was real jealous of her, and they had a big fight—I—that was why
you knocked me all of a heap, when you told me he was dead—I
thought for a minute Nonie's guy did it, and what a stinking mess
that'd be, only then I saw it couldn't be because they were already
gone.

"He wanted to marry her, see. And it was a chance for—just everything. He was making thirty Gs a year, she said. She'd have to learn
how to sort of keep up with him, she wasn't ashamed of being what
she was, of us, but she said to me, she wanted to make it a clean
break—for just a while. Till they—till she got settled down, till after
they were married, see."

"I see," said Jesse. "What about Josie?"

"Well"—she took a long breath—"that was part of it. A girl—I
mean, even when Nonie really liked him, I guess a man wouldn't understand, but you're working on a guy, you plan this and that. She'd
told him about the kid, about Joe walking out, kind of feeding him
how tough she'd had it. And right off, when they got engaged, he
said she ought to have her own baby back, he'd be real glad to have
a little daughter. I—don't figure she'd told him—just how long it'd
been," said Christine rather miserably. "But they'll have to sort that
out themselves. Anyway, that was how it was. They were going to
get married, and take the kid. And she said, a real new start—everything back of her wiped out, forget it, and a while later—when they
were all settled—she'd keep in touch and let me know where they
were living. And that was it."

"Did she tell you his name?" asked Jesse.

She lit a new cigarette from the stub of her latest one. "She didn't
mean to, it slipped out. Just, Carson. You see, Mr. Falkenstein, I
knew how she felt. A real new start. Him crazy about her, and he really wanted the baby, a ready-made family she said he said—I—if she
hadn't already told him about the kid, I don't figure that'd have
mattered to her, but she had and he wanted it so that was that. And
it was a chance at the good life, nice house and a husband really
amounted to something, and—"

"Did she say where they were going to live?"

The hand that held her cigarette was trembling slightly. "No," said Christine. "That was all. And it wasn't that she was ashamed of us, but she said he was, well, a square kind of guy, strait-laced about some things, and she just thought, till they got settled down—"

Jesse let a little silence go by. She fidgeted with the red plastic bracelet on one arm, put out her cigarette, took another out of her gold-mesh case, held it without lighting it. "Mrs. Lefkowitz," he said softly, "did you believe her, about all this?"

She looked at him fleetingly; something like fear flickered in her eyes. "What—do you mean?"

"Is she much of a liar?" asked Jesse. "For any reason? No reason?"

Christine dropped the cigarette, dived blindly after it and sat hunched over for a long minute. Then she straightened up slowly and looked at him. Her wide mouth tightened, she brought out her lighter and lit the cigarette. She was breathing quickly. "Nonie," she said, "can tell a tale, sure. Damn it, you see things, Mr. Falkenstein. I—you want to know—since then, I wondered about it. It was one reason I didn't tell you, held off coming here. Because—well, she said, like a fairy tale, and it sure was, how likely is a girl like Nonie, get a chance like that— But listen, Mr. Falkenstein. Listen, look at it this way. Why would she tell me all that if it wasn't so? What was the point—that's what I finally told myself, see?"

It was, he thought, a point she had. And this would, when he came to think, answer a good many questions. If all that hadn't been so, why had Nonie come out with it to big sister?

"I just decided you'd better hear about it. Because of those people." She got up suddenly and turned to the door, and was gone before he could get up, think of more questions.

The phone shrilled on his desk and he picked it up. "It's Mr. Galen," said Jean.

Jesse said eagerly into the phone, "Galen. Have you got anything?"

"I talked to Bill in Miami ten minutes ago. He had a routine message for the *Princess Pat*'s captain, and slipped your query to the purser tacked onto it. The reply came through last night. Seems your hunch is way off, Mr. Falkenstein. The purser says this Pierce guy's the real life of the party, very popular with the other passengers. The woman with him, supposed to be Mrs. Pierce, is a cute blond, but her name's Rita. And there's no child anywhere on board."

"Oh, really," said Jesse. "I'm very much obliged, Galen. Thanks so much." He put the phone down and swiveled around to stare out the window again.

EIGHT

Borderline, DeWitt said. The reams of solid hard evidence, and who read it any more? But so much that came, damn the form or the means, was borderline. So much maybe and if, symbolical, and/or possibly to be explained by those two old bugbears of the whole field of psychic research, telepathy and the subconscious mind.

If there was such a thing as that.

But there it was, at the back of his conscious mind, a small insistent knocking. That tape.

Tell Jesse, danger to the child.

Abruptly he swiveled around to the desk and met the enigmatic dark eyes of More on the opposite wall. So what about this tale? Smart, rudimentarily shrewd Chris had only half believed it, hesitated to tell, but it provided some answers: it did indeed. Why Nonie had taken Josie even though she hadn't really wanted her. Why she hadn't been back to pick up that money. Why McAllister had had a fight with her. And, of course, there was the last point: Nonie scarcely beyond making up a tale, for whatever reason, but what would have been the point, voluntarily telling that tale to big sister?

Jesse brushed tobacco off the desk, carefully lit a cigarette, reached for the phone and dialed the Wilcox Street precinct. "Sergeant Clock there?" In a moment Clock's voice spoke in his ear. "Andrew, you talked to people McAllister knew. Was there a Ken something among 'em?"

"What? Wait a minute. Pete!" Voices indistinguishable in the background and then Clock came back on. "Yeah, that's right, a Ken Adler, why? The address? Just a minute." He sounded harried. "Now what are you up to? It's Bonner Drive in West Hollywood."

"Thanks." Jesse hung up the phone, got up and went out to the anteroom. "Might as well enjoy the vacation when it comes along, girls. You needn't take any appointments for a while."

The block on Bonner Drive was all garish, new small apartments. The one he wanted was at the rear of a corner lot, an angular modern building painted black and orange. He waited so long after pushing the bell he thought nobody was there, but eventually the door opened and a woman looked at him rather blearily. She was a tall thin blond with a blue robe belted around her, and she looked as if she had a hangover.

"Mrs. Adler," said Jesse, and she nodded. "You own a place at the beach?"

"Nope. Rented one this summer"—she yawned widely at him— "give parties in, weekends, like that. Why—who the hell are you anyway?"

She looked fairly stupid, and he couldn't explain too economically why he was here. Jesse said gently, "There was some question of damage. The real estate agent—"

She came wide awake. "They're crazy, maybe a few cigarette burns, but nothing big! You from Keogh Realty? Well, you tell 'em they don't take us for anything, claim we did any damage, and anyhow they'd have to see my husband about it, not me." She slammed the door.

And lawyers were sometimes hampered by the law, but they had natural weapons that could be useful with the ordinary citizens. Jesse found the Keogh Realty Company on Beverly Boulevard, got in to see one of the partners, told him a tale about a contested divorce hearing and was reluctantly given the address of the beach place the Adlers had rented in Redondo Beach.

It was a wild-goose chase. He drove down there to look over the terrain.

This wasn't classy beach territory, like Malibu or Playa del Rey or Palos Verdes. It was one of the older beach towns, and on the sea side of the coast highway, as along that whole stretch of once beautiful natural bay, the ramshackle little jerry-built houses stood cheek by jowl, and on the other side the narrow old streets held more. Looking for the street name, he drove slowly south on the coast highway; before he found it, the scenery changed slightly, and when he parked in front of the right address, he let out a slow breath, studying it. It was empty and for rent, a two-bedroom cottage on a thirty-foot lot, others of like type on either side, but in the next block up, the lots were wider, the houses newer; and on up from there was a new subdivision, more expensive places. The beach across the highway was unfenced along here, a public beach.

It was also crowded in August during a heat wave; cars were parked in solid phalanxes in all the occasional big lots across the highway. After a search he found a place to leave the car, no street parking here; he walked back to the cottage the Adlers had rented and thought vaguely to himself, serendipity. He hadn't any clue as to where to start. He didn't even know for sure that the wild goose was there, had ever been there. It was very unlikely, if it was there, that he could track it down. But give it the old college try anyway.

The places along this block were the kind of cottages that were rented out by the week, the month. If the wild goose was as described, not likely he'd been anywhere here. Jesse walked up to the next block, where the slightly newer homes were more apt to have permanent residents. With a mental sigh, he pushed the first doorbell and faced a plump housewife. "I'm looking for a man named Carson. I wonder if you could tell me—"

At one-thirty, four and a half blocks up the beach, he veered down to the beach itself to buy a hamburger from a vendor. There were dozens of side streets running down toward the beach, with rows and rows of houses along them. It would take an army of private eyes to cover them all. Chewing the hamburger, he eyed the bikini-clad revelers on the beach with a jaundiced eye. There wasn't the slightest breeze off the water, and the breakers were drifting in very low and easy, as if they'd been slowed down by the heat wave too.

On up from there were fewer crowds; bigger homes right down close to the beach, as the bay curved a little to the east anticipating the class of Playa del Rey farther ahead. A couple of hundred yards up was a sign that said PRIVATE BEACH.

He must have talked briefly to a hundred and fifty householders; and what had he expected? What the hell was he doing here? If the wild goose had ever been anywhere around here, he needn't have left a trace behind at all. The transients coming and going: and one reason people rented beach cottages was to invite other people there, the weekend parties, picnics, casual bashes.

To reach the newer houses abutting on that private beach he had to leave the view of the breakers, turn up a curving wider street where the houses fronted. By that time, he felt he'd been at this for years, plodding from house to house, street to street, the merciless sun beating down, and hearing the same monotonous answers to the monotonous question. This had been one of the least brilliant ideas he'd ever had, the heat wave had addled his wits, and while he still had the strength left he'd better plod back to the car, which must be miles away by now, and go home, or at least somewhere else where there was air conditioning.

He plodded up to the gray-slab front porch of another house and pushed the bell. It was four forty-five. He pushed it again, heard the chimes sound emptily inside, decided nobody was home and went back to the street. A car was just pulling into the drive alongside, which belonged to the next house down. A man got out of it and looked at him.

"You looking for the Fosters? They're back east, supposed to be home next week."

"Actually," said Jesse, "I'm looking for somebody named Carson. A man. I doubt if he lives anywhere here, he could have been someone's guest, overnight or at a party—couple of months ago maybe."

"Oh, I see," said the man doubtfully.

"Know it sounds vague. Very frustrating. I'm a lawyer, hunting for a witness in a—mmh—rather important case. All I've got is the general area and the one name."

"I'll be damned," said the man thoughtfully. He was a cheerful-looking stout man in his forties, dressed in well-tailored sports clothes. "Carson. Young, old, rich, poor? Fat or thin?"

"I've got no idea," said Jesse. "I think I'll forget it and go find some air conditioning."

A woman had come out of the back door at the side of the house and walked down the drive, a woman some years younger than the man, with a reasonably good figure in slacks and halter bra. "Well, you're early. Who's this?"

"A lawyer. Marion, you remember that party last June? Bob asking if he could bring this fellow, and there was such a mob anyway you said it didn't matter? Wasn't his name Carson?"

"Heavens, I don't remember. Something like that, I think. Mob was right, I didn't say more than hello and good-bye to most of them."

"I think it was Carson," said the man. "It was a crowd all right, but I remember talking to him for about half an hour, he was a very nice fellow—interesting. I know it struck me at the time, people not always what you expect."

"What exactly do you mean?" Jesse didn't believe in this kind of happenstance.

"Oh, he was a solid quiet sort of fellow around forty, ordinary-looking, and he was an airline pilot. I don't know where Bob met him. Funny I should run into you just now. You suppose that could be your witness?"

◎◎◎

They were yelling at each other again, and they didn't hear Josie at all.

"It was your great big idea, sounded just fine, but we haven't seen any bread yet—how long's it going to be, anyway?"

"I don't know, I tell you, they keep saying they can't contact him, and at first I thought it was level but now I think they're stalling."

"Well, I'm not hangin' around forever, be a jailer to a kid, without seein' a dime. And what about afterwards anyway? Just like I said—"

"Please," said Josie, trying to say it louder. Denny had the electric fan on in the living room, but it was so hot all her clothes were sticking to her, and the hollow feeling inside seemed to be getting bigger and bigger. The TV was on in here too, turned up loud, and it seemed to echo in her head. Ever since last night, the choking feeling coming back every little while, and there'd been spaghetti, she couldn't eat any with all the yellow cheese on it, and this morning the milk had had something wrong with it so she couldn't eat the cereal. "Please."

Mama was almost ready to go. "What do you want now? My God, why I ever got into this—"

"Please, I think I better have some of the medicine," said Josie. "Mother Sue knows what it is. I don't have to have it very often re-

ally, not for a long time, but when it feels like I can't breathe good
—"

Mama hadn't listened at all. "I'll *get* to them," she said, mad
and loud. "Don't worry, I'll get to them—we'll get the payoff." She
banged the door after her.

The doctor had said she'd probably outgrow it in time, and she
hadn't had it in a long while now, only once after that awfullest
time the firemen had to come and put the thing over her face. But
the feeling was there now, tight inside her chest, and the spark of
terror—if it came, like dark and thunder, she couldn't breathe, she
felt all over again how it was when it came—and Mother Sue wasn't
there, none of the little white pills that helped— *They* wouldn't do
anything, and she'd probably die. If it came, and she couldn't
breathe, she'd just die.

"*Please*," she said to Denny. He was scowling, all red in the face,
looking mad. "Please, I better have the medicine. You can call
Mother Sue and she'd tell you what it is. I think—"

"What the hell's a little kid want with medicine?" said Denny,
not really paying attention. "Listen, kid, I got a lot on my mind,
don't bother me today, huh? You go watch some cartoons on TV or
something, nothing on I want to see till the sportcast." He went into
the bathroom and shut the door, and after a minute Josie heard the
shower start.

She stood there feeling all hollow and something in her head like
a balloon blowing up and then getting little again, and the ache that
was almost the beginning of the choking feeling was one big *I want
to go home*— Blindly she went over to the door and it opened and
she was out of the apartment, running down the hall. Stairs—she
remembered the way they'd gone before, when Denny took her out.
Three, five, six flights of stairs, and then the front door and the
street. She ran, panting, and had to slow down, afraid he was coming
after her. She wasn't sure which way that main street was—just
houses and apartments here, and it was so hot, like the street and
the houses couldn't breathe either. She tried to run again, and just
up there a block away felt a small surge of triumph—she was going
to get home, somehow she was going to get home—

If she could ask the way, which way is Kingsley Street, she could
start to walk— But her head felt so queer, and the hollow feeling

kept getting bigger, and if the choking feeling really came, she couldn't walk—it might be an awful long way, Los Angeles was a big place—

She saw a woman sitting on the bench at the corner there, and went up to her and asked, "Please, which way is Kingsley Street from here?" The woman smiled at her politely and said something quick and funny *No sé, no sé.* Well, if she wasn't going to say—Josie looked back and thought she saw Denny coming, and her heart jumped and she tried to run again. Then all of a sudden, right up ahead, she saw that place—Lew's Bar—where Denny had taken her that day, and she thought dizzily, some of the other men had been nice, smiled and joked at her—if they'd let her use the phone, or maybe if she asked someone would give her a dime for the phone if it was a pay one, and she could call home and Daddy Fred would come—

The phone number. She knew her own phone number, it was easy to remember—she *had* to remember it, she was so near now—she sobbed desperately, groping after it, like the prayers, maybe God's so mad He'd never let her remember— But the phone number slid into her head smooth and easy and she began saying it over, running as fast as she could toward that door.

It was dark and smelled the same. She stumbled up to the long counter. The same man was there with the white apron. "Please," said Josie, "may I use your phone, please, I want to call home."

"What?" said the man. He peered at her over the counter. "Clear outta here," he said. "Go on, beat it! Kids not allowed in here."

"I just want to use your phone, it wouldn't take a minute—" But he'd turned away, he didn't hear her.

"What's the matter, dear?" asked another voice. Josie turned, feeling dizzy, and it was the other man, the one named Don, who'd been nice that day.

"I just want—to call home," she said faintly. "On the phone. I haven't got a dime, but if I could just—"

"Why, sure, sweetie," said Don. He was running his hand all up her arm, patting it. "Sure, I'll take you someplace there's a phone you can use." He was squeezing her shoulder now, a little too hard. "Listen, you can come to my place, I got a nice apartment right close, there's a phone and you won't need a dime, how's that?"

"Oh, would you, please—" His hand felt funny, but Josie was so grateful she didn't care. He could tell her where to tell Daddy Fred to come—she clutched at his arm frantically, seeing home so close, so easy—

"What the hell you think you're doing, mister?"

"Me? Nothing," said Don. "Nothing. I just like kids."

The apron man leaned over the counter. "I can see that," he said in an ugly voice. "You get outta this place, I don't need your kind around. Kid, you beat it, I said! Gwan, get out! And you go before him!"

"You can't order me around," said Don. "I'm not doing anything."

The apron man came out from behind the counter and took Josie's arm and pulled her to the door. "You go on home, for gossakes. Kids! Queers! Gwan!"

Josie stumbled out onto the street, hating him fiercely—just another minute and Don would have taken her where there was a phone—she'd nearly had it in her hand, Mother Sue, I want to come home, I want to come home—

It wasn't time for it to get dark yet, but it was—she couldn't see very clear, and she was afraid she'd fall down. She ran up against somebody and he said, "Watch where you're goin', kid!" She stopped, trying hard to think what to do—ask somebody else which way to go, but if it was all dark she couldn't walk— The only thing in her head at all was home, home, home—

And Denny said roughly, "What the hell you think you're doin'?" He grabbed her by one arm and shook her. "Run out like that, make me chase you to hellengone—"

"Let me go," whispered Josie. "Please let me go. I want to go home."

"That's where you're goin'," he said. "Come on. Can't you walk, for God's sake? What the hell's wrong with you? Oh, hell—" And he picked her up and started to carry her, walking fast. He was awful strong, he smelled of shave lotion like Daddy Fred used sometimes only a different kind. There was a kind of mist all around, Josie could see other people in the street, hear the cars, people all around, but nobody paying any attention, taking any notice, and she couldn't do anything but whisper over and over, "*Please, please, please—*"

◎◉◎

Jesse didn't believe in this kind of luck, but there it was: the one incredible break. By the time he got back to Hollywood it was too late to follow up on it, but he got into the office early on Wednesday morning and set the Gordons to working on it along with him.

"There can't be many airlines to cover. Split them up," he said, leafing through the Yellow Pages. "More than you might think—"

"And you don't know it's one of the big ones," said Jean.

"There'll be dozens altogether," said Jimmy. "All the local ones, there must be dozens going up and down the coast, as well as all the big ones, United , Eastern, PanAm, American—"

"Don't throw wet blankets," said Jesse. "After that kind of break, we're bound to find him. Come on, let's start talking to personnel departments."

It was Jimmy who found him, an hour and a half later, and interrupted Jesse as he was talking to personnel at West Coast Airways. "Here he is. It was Continental." She laid a memo slip on the desk. It said Vincent Carson, captain, Continental Airlines. Jesse looked at it with awe; after the break, he'd know they had to find him, but it was still a chancy thing. "They wouldn't part with an address, said it wasn't company policy, but if it was a legal matter you could see the chief of personnel personally. It's Hollywood Way in Burbank."

"I'd go a hell of a lot farther than that," said Jesse, "to get Mr. Carson's address. Thanks, Jimmy." He bolted out and downstairs.

At the severely modern fieldstone and glass building on Hollywood Way, he had to wait to see the chief of personnel, a Walter Butler. When he was finally let into Butler's office, he heard a little lecture. "It's just that we can't go handing out private addresses to any Tom, Dick or Harry, you can appreciate that, Mr. Falkenstein. But if, as you say, it's a question of this sort—you're looking for Carson as a witness—accident, damage suit, something like that?—I must say I'm surprised you didn't *have* his address, if it was a police matter—"

"Client very confused," said Jesse meekly, "wasn't sure which police, sheriff or city. Just heard Carson giving his name and, er, employer."

"Oh, I see. Well, it'll be up to him to deal with it, but I must say I hope it won't come to having to be in court, one of our *pilots*, we have schedules to maintain—" Butler summoned a steno and dispatched her to look up the address. "You're lucky that Carson does live locally, as I recall. Not all our pilots do. And he may not be available at once. I don't recall offhand which flight he's on now, but if it's one of the longer ones—east, or Hawaii—there'll be a layover at the other end, two or three days as a rule."

"Yes. He been with Continental long?"

"As I recall, ten or twelve years—he's one of our senior captains, of course." It was polite conversation. The steno came back with a memo slip and gave it to Butler, who passed it to Jesse. "There you are. Oh, no trouble—sorry you were put to the inconvenience of coming down, but you can understand that we have to be careful."

"I'm very much obliged," said Jesse truthfully. He didn't glance at the slip until he was back in the Dodge.

It said, Grandero Drive, Yorba Linda.

On the freeway, it wasn't that long a drive out to the wilds of Orange County. It was, of course, a good ten degrees hotter out there. The street was on the outskirts of town, a curving wide street of spacious houses about ten years old, well-kept houses with manicured lawns, good-sized yards. About seventy thousand average, thought Jesse, and taxes to match. A step up for Nonie all right. Some of the answers were dovetailing in his mind. He was still feeling slightly incredulous that this wild, wild goose had been tracked down at all.

The address he wanted was at the end of a block, a tan stucco and brick house with a wide expanse of front lawn. He left the Dodge at the curb, went up and pushed the bell.

The woman who opened the door was middle-aged, thin, gray-haired and sharp-faced. "Yay-uss?" she asked, looking at Jesse warily. "We don't buy at the door."

"Not selling anything. I'm looking for Captain Carson." Jesse gave her a card.

She looked at it. "Lawyer. Well, he doesn't need one now and I only hope he won't need one later on. Anyway, you can't see him. I'm just the help, house-sitting." The minute he'd seen her, he'd thought she was nursing a grievance, and it was all ready to come out to anybody handy to talk to. "I've looked after this place four days a week and oblige for cooking at parties, ever since they lived here. Mis' Carson the nicest lady I ever worked for, always pleasant-spoken, please, thank you, a real lady. I cried my eyes out. Just terrible. I only hope he knows what he's doing, but with a man that isn't likely. It was just a tragedy, poor lady."

"Er—a divorce?" asked Jesse.

"She *died*," said the woman indignantly. "Only thirty-two, poor soul, this awful cancer. She took and died inside of three months, that was only last year and I looked for him to sell the house but he didn't. He could afford to keep it of course, makes big money. Flies airplanes to Honolulu and New York, all over. Well, all I will say is, he did wait a year—I'll give him that—but men! I haven't laid eyes on this one, but what he said— Well, I can see as far through a piece of glass as anybody."

"Oh. He waited a year—"

"To marry somebody else. Poor sweet lady, I'm sure she'd wish him to be happy if she wasn't peaceful at rest till Judgment Day as we all know, but from what I've heard I don't expect it." She sounded gloomily pleased. "Mis' Stanley, he says, that bein' my name, the new Mrs. Carson's pretty young and not used to managing a house, I'm sure you'll help her, he says. Been used to living right in town, he says, be a different life for her. Showed me a picture—and if you ask me it'll be different all right. Little blond chit in a skirt over her knees, can't be more'n twenty-five, and him forty if he's a day and a settled man. All I say is, it's a good thing him and Mis' Carson never had any children, though she wanted 'em and so did he, he *said*."

"That's very interesting," said Jesse. "Do you expect him in soon?"

"Why, I don't expect him at all," she said. "Aren't I just telling you? He's just got married to this girl and they're off on a honeymoon somewhere. He got two weeks' vacation from flying the airplanes. They're supposed to be back a week from tomorrow."

On Thursday morning Clock was reading a lab report on the latest burglary when he got a buzz from the desk. "A citizen," said the desk sergeant laconically, "with a tip." He put the citizen through, and Clock said, "Sergeant Clock."

"Listen," said a heavy male voice, "I don't want to get anybody in trouble but also I don't like the kooks. I'm Joe Wagner, bartender down here at Lew's on Adams. There's a guy been dropping in here, I think he's a kook. I've—uh—seen him making up to the kids on the playground, you know, the little girls, pattin' 'em and sweet-talking. And—uh—another kid, little girl, right out in the street here. I think he's one of them nuts, know what I mean."

"You know his name?" asked Clock.

"Just Don. But I don't want that kind in my place, and if he is that kind he hadn't ought to be running around loose. I don't suppose this is enough for you to arrest him, but I thought I'd pass it on."

"You might be surprised," said Clock. "You know where he lives?"

"No, but he's in here now if you want to talk to him. Drinkin' a beer."

"Isn't that nice," said Clock. "Sit tight, and thanks very much." He got the desk. "Steve, chase a unit down to Lew's bar on Adams—it's possible Lightner's there waiting to be picked up." He relayed that to Petrovsky and Mantella. "Any guesses about the public-spirited citizen?"

Mantella smiled thoughtfully. "Who isn't apt to be standing around playgrounds much of the time. Sure. Maybe his own kid, or the kid of some friend, said something about this character, and nobody wants any publicity, the kids questioned by cops. Six of one, half dozen of another. If it is Lightner, at least we'll have him."

It was Lightner. The Traffic men fetched him in twenty minutes later, and Clock was ferociously pleased to see him. He hunched his wide shoulders at Lightner and said pleasantly, "So we catch up to you again, you slimy bastard. I hope this time they'll throw the key away."

"You can't talk to me like that."

"You just heard me. Did you give him his rights?" The Traffic men said they had. "So that's all according to Hoyle. Pete, take him away somewhere, I'll be with you in a minute." As Petrovsky led Lightner off to an interrogation room, Clock thought tiredly, The games we have to play. That was the oldest, and the funny thing was

that Lightner knew it, but he might fall for it anyway. Petrovsky
would be the amiable, friendly cop, soft-talking and promising possible leniency for a statement, Clock the old-fashioned heavy breathing threats, and between them they might break him down.

It took two hours. "What about the Staples girl, Don?" Over and
over. "We've got two witnesses who'll identify you. By God, I'd like
to beat you up for that one, for two cents I'd—"

"Ah, give him a chance, Andrew. You know, Don, there'd likely
be a reduced plea if you co-operate here—"

"Don't talk so soft to the bastard! You caught that little girl on
her way home from the movies, you said you'd give her a puppy and
you got her behind that billboard along Fountain—" That was
where, in the classic tradition, Lightner should have said it wasn't either, it was Edgmont, but he didn't. "Come on, Lightner, we all
know you did it, and the other little girl too, come on, come on, tell
us about it, you bastard—" Clock felt a little sick, thinking about
the Staples girl, looking at Lightner, this mild-appearing man, a thin
gray man with professorial-looking glasses. The Staples girl had had
to have surgery, and the doctors said she'd probably never be able to
have children. Not all the bullying and swearing was play-acting, but
it just relieved his own feelings.

"The quicker you decide to be reasonable, the quicker we can stop
all this," said Petrovsky easily. "Come on, Don, we all know it was
you."

"All right, all right, all right!" he shouted at them eventually. "So
it was me! You can't do anything to me, I'm just sick, that's all—
that's what the head doctors say, I'm *sick*—you can't do anything!"

"The Staples child," said Clock tiredly. "Pin it down, Don. Two
weeks ago last night, Edgmont and Fountain, about eight o'clock."

"All right, all right, yes! But you can't do anything. I'm sick!" he
said triumphantly.

They found keys on him, a wallet, an address and they went to
have a look there: a single rented room in a hotel on Adams. Among
other things, they found the belt of the Staples girl's dress, with
some blood on it, and a worn pair of girl's panties. The other little
girl had come home with her panties missing; maybe the mother
could identify these. They called up the lab to poke around for more
possible evidence, but what they had was enough.

"And I hope to God," said Clock savagely, "that they'll hang onto him this time! Goddamn, Pete, look at his pedigree—and the courts hand him a one-to-three at the most, he's out in six months roaming the streets looking for more little girls! What the hell good is it for us to catch them when the courts take the reduced plea to save time or let 'em out on P.A. inside a year—"

"Don't raise my blood pressure, Andrew. It's bad enough with the heisters and burglars," said Petrovsky. "But the ones like Don—it's the kids always get you. The innocent bystanders with a vengeance."

◎◎◎

"It's her, Mr. Quiller—will you take it?"

They were alone in the office. He came in a hurry out of the inner office, said, "Put it on the amplifier, baby."

Lorna transferred the phone, and the voice suddenly filled the room. "—better do something about it, see? I'm overdue for some of that bread, you got the proof of that, and I want what's coming. You know the stink I can make."

Quiller muttered, "Not like in other days, baby, but we know."

"What the hell's the delay? I told you, tell him—"

"Listen, doll." He raised his voice to register on the line. "We can't get to him, I told you that. He'll be back any day now. He'll pay up. You give me a number we can reach you when he gets here, see?"

"Don't call me, I'll call you, mister. He better get back, he better come through." The phone at the other end was slammed down.

Quiller raised his eyes to heaven. "Someday," he said, "someday, baby, I'm goin' to quit this rat race and buy a farm a hundred miles from the big city and just vegetate."

Lorna didn't say, that'll be the day; she just thought it.

◎◎◎

Josie had lain in the dark struggling with terror, with the savage sharp pain, a nightmare of an unknown time. Outgrow it said the doctor and such a long time since the choking feeling so bad and if it started to come just a little Mother Sue and the little white pills—

EATS EATS EATS said the sign. It was so hot nobody could breathe when it was so hot but only Josie had the pain like a knife cutting off her breath forgot to say her prayers naturally God didn't like it tried to remember tried to remember Our Father who art and here nobody to bring the pills tried to tell them but they don't care I want to go home I want to go home I want to go home—

In a vast roaring distance somewhere Josie was aware of noise, a rasping harsh noise, and dimly knew it was her own noise, the awful, final, savage struggle to breathe.

◎◎◎

The man and woman faced each other, and they were both fright-ened; they met the fright in each other's eyes.

"What the hell?" he said stupidly. "What's wrong with her?"

"I don't know—kids don't have heart attacks, it's like she can't breathe—"

"Listen, we better get a doctor to her. Poor little kid, my God, lis-ten to that, death rattle like—"

"Don't be a fool!" she said. "I know what it is now, only nobody told me the kid had that, and wouldn't you know she'd get it now—damn, damn, damn, everything going wrong—it's what they call asthma, you can't breathe good when you get it—"

"She's goin' to die, she can't breathe, listen, we got to get some help—I can call the fire department, they got all that stuff like oxy-gen and—"

Her hand clamped down on his wrist, hot and hard. "We don't call anybody! I know how that bit goes, they want to take her to the hospital, names and addresses, permission to treat her, that show on TV tells how they do—"

"What the hell?" said the man. In the hot airless room the child's great whooping gasps for breath made punctuation marks to their speech. "What the hell difference—you can tell them you're her mother, they wouldn't ask—"

"No! Listen—" She was breathing hard herself. "There's that all-night drugstore just down the boulevard. You go there, quick, now, and ask them for something. Say it's a kid, and asthma, something to make her breathe better. You *go*, Denny!"

He was panicky, listening to the harsh, rasping, difficult breaths. "My God, what if she passes out on us? What could we do?—a kid —kids don't die, not just little kids—"

"You *go!* Get something—hurry up, for God's sake!"

He was the strong one, physically; and he'd knocked her around a little, when she argued at him; but the chips down, she was the one in charge, decisive and quick. He knew it, and he went out in a hurry.

NINE

Nell woke with a start, automatically expecting to hear the baby yelling; it was a moment before she realized it wasn't her offspring but her husband who had waked her. He was jerking and twisting, uttering loud moans and gasps. Nell put her hand on him. "Jesse!" He just groaned and muttered louder; Nell sat up and fumbled for the lamp switch. She shook him harder. "Jesse, wake up—"

He woke up with a convulsive shudder, and lay still, and she said, "You were having a nightmare, darling. Something chasing you?"

He raised up slowly on one elbow. They'd left the air conditioning on, a hot humid night, but he was perspiring; he wiped his face. "Nightmare?" he said muzzily. "No. I'm all right—I think." He blinked at her in the light. Nell propped herself up higher, found cigarettes on the night table, lit two and gave him one.

"Calm down. Tell me about it and it'll go away."

Jesse shook his head, "Not a nightmare, exactly. So damned real." Gradually he relaxed, exhaling smoke with a long sigh. "Augggh. Nightmare, no—but I saw the old man, Nell. It was a queer place— just bare rocks, and a mist, and there was somebody else there but I couldn't see him—just the old man. Edgar. I saw him as plain as I ever saw him anytime—just the same as always—wrinkled gray suit, his tie all crooked, and by God there was even a bottle in his breast pocket, I saw the bulge. He was annoyed with me too, kept saying, not usin' all your brains, Jesse, use the sense God gave you." Jesse shook himself. "It was queer—so damn real. This mist or whatever it was started to close in, and I was trying to tell him, just doing my best, Edgar—but it wasn't all the mist, it was like a telephoto shot, he was getting farther and farther away, miles away but I could still see him plain, and the fog closing in, and I could hear him shouting at me, from miles away. Then ask Mack, he was shouting, then ask

Mack—" Jesse drew strongly on the cigarette. "Glad you woke me up. Don't know why I should have been so shook, but it was so real. Not so surprising I should dream about him, I suppose—been thinking of him—Dangerfield's red tape—wondering what he'd say about this business."

Nell looked at him thoughtfully. "Isn't it?" she said. "I wonder, Jesse. Some of what I've been reading—a lot of dreams you can explain, associations or just indigestion, but some of them are real. Astral travel. Don't they say, your conscious inhibitions blocked off, so —the other side can get through, or—sometimes—you get across there."

Jesse slid down against the pillow. "I can still see him, damn it. He'll have more important things to do with himself than getting at me in a dream."

"Then ask Mack," said Nell. "That's plain enough, Jesse. Go ask MacDonald. He knew MacDonald, after all."

Jesse stared at her. "Well, I suppose that would have occurred to me eventually. I did think once I was about ready to ask some psychic help on this one. Go back to sleep, lady—at least the baby's quiet and we can."

Nell turned off the light, but said into the darkness, "I think it was real, Jesse. Maybe you had better go ask MacDonald."

Jesse grunted and put the pillow over his head.

◎◎◎

But, facing himself in the shaving mirror next morning, he wondered. The curious thing was, he thought he'd finished his hunt for Nonie now; it was just a question of time. He wanted to see the Lannings today and tell them about that. But there was just the remnant of uneasiness at the back of his mind, and even awake and facing broad daylight he heard a teasing echo of that urgent call, *Ask Mack*.

He swallowed two cups of coffee and left Nell coping with the sleepy baby; he got to the office before the Gordons, and found the manila envelope in the top drawer of the desk: the scrawled illiterate notes from Nonie, the pictures. He heard the Gordons talking to each other, coming in. He picked up the phone and dialed DeWitt's apartment.

"You expecting MacDonald into your headquarters today, William?"

"What? You're an early bird. Charles? Yes, it's his day off, he's got a couple of appointments this morning. Don't tell me you want one."

"When'll he be in? Nine? I'll be there," said Jesse. He considered the envelope. MacDonald, a plain intelligent man; like most serious psychics, not given to the mumbo-jumbo. And a gifted psychometrist. But so much of it was, as you might say, delicately balanced: on border lines. Jesse found two more envelopes; he put the notes in one, and the two pictures in the other, sealed them and put them in his pocket.

The inexpensive quarters DeWitt had found for his researches were in an old office building on Santa Monica Boulevard: three big rooms on the second floor, and two small connecting offices. Two of the rooms had been carpeted and fitted out with ordinary furniture, for the psychics' sittings; DeWitt had his far-out tape machines in the third, where the file cabinets were beginning to accumulate too. He wasn't there when Jesse arrived, but the plain, spectacled Miss Duffy greeted him, looking surprised.

"Mr. MacDonald? Why, yes, he's just come in, but he's got a sitting in half an hour—"

"Hope it won't take him that long to perform for me," said Jesse. "I'll pay the regular fee if you like."

"Goodness, that's not necessary, Mr. Falkenstein, you keeping all our books—you go right in." She still looked surprised.

Jesse went into the first of the two rooms, looking like anybody's comfortable study: couch, chairs, a long table. Charles MacDonald was sitting at the table. He was a dark, thin, youngish man with stooped shoulders, grave-eyed and grave-mouthed. In private life—or, Jesse thought, in public life—he worked for the city as an electrician. He looked up as Jesse entered. "Well, I didn't expect to see you, Mr. Falkenstein."

"Coming to see the animals perform?" Jesse smiled and sat down across the table from him. "I know better than to tell you why, or what I might expect to hear from you. Just tell me what comes to you about this," and he laid the first envelope on the table between them.

MacDonald laid one hand on it and shut his eyes. As a psychometrist, he made no effort at the trance state; he had a high reputation for accuracy, but his clairvoyance was not, Jesse remembered, straightforward. After a moment he said, "Nothing. It's all dark—just a little light in the far distance, but a long way off. I'm sorry, I just don't get anything out of this at all. A blank wall."

"Well. Try this," and Jesse put the other envelope down.

MacDonald picked it up, turning it over in his long hands without looking at it. "Why, it's New York," he said, and instantly added, "No, that's wrong, I don't know why I said that. There's money involved here, a lot of money. Where is she, no, where are they—that's what you want to know. There isn't much coming through about that, it's not clear. The money, yes. Greed for money—someone greedy for money—but it's coming in some wrong way." He was silent, and then he laughed. "This really sounds very silly, but it's the strongest picture I get, I'd better describe it—it looks like a group of —of dignitaries, politicians, men in very formal dress, striped trousers and flowers in their buttonholes. A rose by any other name—any other name. And there's danger coming with the money."

He laid the envelope down and looked at Jesse. "Not much," he said. "I'm sorry. Not what you expected?"

"Didn't expect anything," said Jesse. "I don't know what to expect, MacDonald. But thanks anyway."

"I never do either. I do wonder," said MacDonald interestedly, "what that means, all those politicians with carnations. Funny. You're worried about something."

"You haven't helped any," said Jesse.

He saw the Lannings at home. "Speak about private eyes, no professional ever got such a break—it was a chance in a million, you can see that. It looks very much as if Nonie has captured herself a prosperous husband, and is off enjoying a honeymoon. I'm bound to tell you, and I'm sorry, doesn't look as if the chances are good for you to get Josie back, if that's so. You can see how this fits, answers questions."

Lanning just nodded dumbly, but his wife sat forward in her chair. "But, Mr. Falkenstein—I see that—what you said about his wanting a family and once she'd told him about Josie, she had to come for her even when she didn't want to. But why *then?* They wouldn't take her with them on their honeymoon!"

"No. I was going on to that, Mrs. Lanning. I talked to the neighbor on one side as well as this Mrs. Stanley. Carson's got a sister living here, a family of her own, and it occurs to me, it could be they've left Josie with her until they get back. Also occurred to me—you said there was no word about where to send clothes and so on—that he'd have said something like, buy her everything new. The sister's a Mrs. Randolph Goss, I got the address and phone number from the Stanley woman but I haven't been able to reach her yet."

"Oh. Where does she live?"

"Thousand Oaks. The husband's a C.P.A., according to Mrs. Stanley—sound like prosperous people, eminently respectable."

"Mr. Falkenstein"—her eyes were bright on him—"couldn't we just go there? Now? If Josie's there—she didn't give me a chance to tell her anything about Josie, there's a list of her allergies, and the antihistamine prescription, and—I know, I realize we couldn't do anything, expect anything, but at least this woman sounds—more sensible than Nonie, and I'd just like—please, if you were with us, wouldn't it be all right?"

"Well—" Jesse thought perhaps they deserved that much. "I was going out there myself. Don't see what harm it could do—set your mind at rest."

"I'll get my bag. I'll take the prescription, and the list." She hurried out.

Lanning looked after her and said, "She'll go on hoping till the bitter end."

"Maybe we all do that, Mr. Lanning."

He drove them out through the hot valley, once so bare and empty, now sprouting new towns and glittering shopping centers and even the office-building complexes. Thousand Oaks was, largely, solid money: new houses on large lots, some on one- and two-acre sections with stables; expensive apartments with full security; the kind of mobile-home parks where there was space around each one, landscaping. The address they wanted was a house much like Carson's house in Yorba Linda, a big house on a quiet residential street.

Lanning put a hand on his wife's arm, or she'd have run ahead of them up to the door. But they waited, hearing the chimes inside, and the door stayed shut.

"Padlock on the garage," said Jesse. In the inner city it might not say much: might not even here, everybody conscious of the crime wave. "I wonder—August, after all. We might ask." The Lannings followed him to the house next door, another newly painted expensive house. They waited on the porch, and the door opened. "We're looking for the Gosses," said Jesse. "Next door. Can you tell us if they're away?"

She looked at them curiously, a middle-aged woman with graying dark hair, pleasant eyes. "Why, yes," she said, "they are. We don't know them very well, we've just moved here, but I've spoken to her several times, I know that. Mr. Goss's vacation started a couple of weeks ago, he's taking a month. They rented a camper and were going to drive over to the Grand Canyon, maybe up to Zion National Park afterward. Mrs. Goss said they thought it'd be educational for the children."

"The children?" said Mrs. Lanning eagerly. "How many?"

"They've got two of their own. Two girls about seven and ten. But why—"

"Oh, please, it's just that we've got to know—was there another little girl—"

"We were wondering," said Jesse quickly, "if, er, my friend here's little niece was with them—Mrs. Lanning, er, Mrs.—?"

"Boyce," she said. "I'm Mrs. Boyce."

"The Lannings are just visiting here for a short time," said Jesse, feeling his way, "and her sister is in the hospital—unconscious— she'd said something about her little girl being off with friends, and we'd like to—"

It wasn't a very good effort on the spur of the moment, but seemed to serve. Mrs. Boyce thawed slightly. "Oh, I see. Well, that was probably it, then. If they're friends of your sister's, Mrs. Lanning. I thought at the time, one of the little girl's friends. I did notice, that morning they drove off, there were three children. Scampering in and out of the camper, you know, all excited."

"A little girl nearly nine," said Mrs. Lanning, her hands clutching each other tightly. "Thin, with curly dark hair."

"I couldn't say, I'm sure. I just noticed. I think the other one was in between the Goss's children in size."

"You were right then," said Mrs. Lanning, back in the Dodge. "It's a nice house—and what you said about Mr. Carson—" She let out a long breath. "I just hope, when they do get back, they'd let us see Josie sometimes. It'll all be so strange to her—and I don't care, that woman doesn't want her. Even though he has money, I just can't see Josie being happy. I only hope these people are taking good care—" She began to cry a little in a tired way, and Jesse started the car in silence. They were both sitting in the back seat; he heard Lanning soothing her.

As he got back on the freeway, he said, "I want to see Mrs. Stanley again, show her Nonie's picture. Just to be sure."

"But—we are sure, aren't we?" said Lanning.

"Probably," said Jesse. It had occurred to him that there was such a thing as coincidence, and in an area where upwards of six and a half milllion people lived— He didn't say that to the Lannings. They had enough to think about right now.

And he was also thinking about what MacDonald had said.

Clock had just finished helping Mantella to lean on one of their heist suspects; nothing definite had come out, they'd had to let him go. He sat down at his desk with a sigh, and the phone rang. It was one of the surgeons at the morgue, Blandish. "You don't usually send us anything so offbeat, Sergeant. It'll be a little while before you get an autopsy report, but I thought I'd alert you."

"What did we send you?"

"Female body found in a car somewhere, last Tuesday."

Clock thought. Guttierez had said something about that. "Yes? What about it?"

"Well, she died of nicotine poisoning. The pure stuff, highly concentrated. We just got the lab report. I've never seen a case before, it isn't a thing you run into every day. We thought you'd like to know."

"That's a funny one all right. I'll pass it on."

"And while I've got you," said Blandish, "I'd better also say that it'll be a lot longer before you get a report on that other one—the one up in the park on Sunday. God, what a mess. I don't know that we'll ever get much out of it, early to say. Of course we can make up a dental chart. At the moment we're doing some analyses on skin tissue to find out whether it's Negro or Caucasian. Though, oddly enough, the stomach wasn't in bad shape, partly mummified, and it may be something will show up—"

"Yes, well, let us know when your final results are in," said Clock hastily; he didn't like even to think about that one. "Thanks Doctor." He looked around; Guttierez was typing a report at his desk. "Hey, *compadre*, it looks as if you've got a real old-fashioned mystery to work. That body in a car—you were on it. Girl seems to have been poisoned with nicotine."

"That is offbeat," agreed Guttierez. "I'm still waiting for something on the car. It was junked, just sitting along Cherokee— Traffic tagged it and spotted the body. No I.D. on the body, no plates, no registration. The garage should have the engine number and serial number by now, but I ask you, where could that lead and how long a hunt would it be? Back to the original manufacturer? It was a 1952 Plymouth."

"Anonymous." Clock nodded. "It could have had twenty owners. But eventually you'd get something."

"I'll believe it when I see it," said Guttierez.

The phone rang again and Clock picked it up. "They're here," said Fran. "They've already got holes knocked in the ceiling in the kitchen and living room. There are five of them—the crew I mean—and the pipes they're going to put in look big enough for the Alaska pipeline."

"Well, good," said Clock.

"And Sally's already bitten one of them—the men I mean—so I've got her tied up at the end of the yard," said Fran.

"And they've got the stove disconnected—in fact all the power is off at the moment—so we're going to Jesse and Nell's for dinner."

"Here, what about breakfast?" asked Clock. "How long is it going to be off?"

"Oh, they said they'd put it back before they left, we just thought it'd be easier to consolidate dinner," said Fran. "You might as well go straight there, I'll walk over. It looks like an awful mess, but they said they'd clear everything up and do the repainting."

◎◎◎

Having driven all the way out to Yorba Linda again, Jesse found Mrs. Stanley absent from the Carson house. The neighbor he'd talked to before said oh, Thursday was her bingo day, she went somewhere and played all day, and no, no idea where.

Jesse went back to his office and stared at some overdue paper work. He had, playing private eye the last couple of days, driven approixmately 250 miles and walked at least ten, and he was feeling lackadaisical. The trouble was, he didn't feel inclined for the purely cerebral effort in contrast. He just sat there awhile, not thinking but feeling—for no really good reason—a little uneasy. A little dissatisfied.

Money. A lot of money. Well, Carson would be doing very well indeed.

Bureaucrats in striped pants.

And six and a half million people—

He found himself yawning. He wished the Dodge was air conditioned, though he didn't often have occasion for long drives. It had been much hotter that far out in the valley.

Those poor damned people. And poor Josie, for that matter. Money not everything.

Queer dream. The old man so real there, looking just as usual. Use your brain, Jesse. Just the way he used to say it. And, ask Mack. MacDonald.

He yawned again, and decided he'd better go home. He wasn't accomplishing anything here; he wasn't sure that he'd accomplished anything, playing private eye.

When he came in the back door, Nell was stirring something on the stove while Athelstane sat behind her looking hopeful. "Fran and Andrew'll be here. They've got the air conditioning people in and the house is all torn up, Fran says. And the electricity off. Jesse —"

"Well?"

"Did you?"

"Did I what?"

"You know perfectly well."

Jesse grinned and kissed her again. "We may as well wait for Fran and Andrew. I think if there's any ESP in the family, Fran's got it."

He was stretched out on the couch in the living room, the girls busy in the kitchen, when Clock arrived; he got up to fix drinks. Nell said she'd stick to sherry and Fran joined her. "I understand," said Fran over her glass, "you had some advice from Edgar, Jesse. Did you take it?"

"For whatever it's worth—I was going to tell you." Under Clock's derisive eye he did.

"Lot of double-talk," said Clock. "You could make it mean anything."

"No, you can't," said Fran seriously. "It's just the same as what he told me that time—the same kind of thing, I mean. When we were all knocking ourselves out to save you from that frame, you materialistic thug. It sounded perfectly meaningless, but when we found out what was behind the frame, it meant something quite—quite specific."

"The trouble is," said Jesse, "it needed the old man's brains to interpret it. I can't make head or tail of this."

"Neither can I right now," said Fran, "but it'll turn out to mean something, Jesse. Only it looks as if you'd already solved your little mystery."

"What strikes me funny," said Clock, "is a man like Carson falling for a cheap blond like Nonie."

"But she's *exactly*"—said both girls together, and Nell went on, —"the type he would, Andrew. A man of that age. Exactly the type that might attract him. Renewing his youth."

"And I might add to that," said Fran thoughtfully, "that it may be early to feel sorry for the Lannings. It's quite possible that Mr. Carson'd get very tired of Nonie in just a little while, and they'll split up. And he wouldn't want Josie."

"Women—leaping miles to conclusions," said Clock.

"I wonder if I have," said Jesse.

"What d'you mean? You said nobody seems to know where they've gone for the honeymoon, but they'll be back sometime."

Jesse was silent. Then he said, "Damn it, it just isn't good enough. I never did cultivate the virtue of patience." He got up and started down the hall, leaving his drink and pursued by Athelstane, who was fascinated with the telephone.

After a session with Information and wrestling with long distance, he got the chief ranger station in Grand Canyon National Park. At least his imagination was getting a workout; he spun a tale, no, no bad news to break but an urgent legal matter—no, he didn't know the make of the camper or the plate number, but if— "Might get them for you, though. I'll try—call you back. . . . Andrew, could you use your status to get the official description of Goss's camper for me?"

"Oh, for God's sake," said Clock. "The rules I break to oblige my nosy brother-in-law." But he called in, got the night watch on it. The Gosses didn't own the camper, but there would have been the inevitable red tape to renting it, a record of Goss's license number and so on; and the D.M.V. had computers now. The reply came back while they were having dinner, and Jesse called the ranger station again.

"Well, we can try to track it down for you," said the ranger dubiously, "but in the middle of the season, this place is a madhouse, hundreds of people camped all over the different grounds. See what we can do is all."

"Thanks very much." Jesse gave him both home and office numbers.

◎◎◎

"Say, we were a little scared about you, kid. You feel better now?"

"I guess," said Josie. She could breathe better, they'd given her the pills after all, not the same but they helped some. But she still felt hollow, and as if she moved too fast or turned too quick it would all come back, the choking and gasping.

"I guess you haven't had much to eat in a while. You want me to get you something?" He stood over her looking like he didn't know what to do; he was trying to be nice again. "Hamburger or a hot dog maybe?"

"No."

"Well—how about some nice fried chicken? I guess there's still some left."

"No, thank you."

"Well, you want anything—" He went out, and she heard the TV go on. She felt the hot slow tears in her eyes, not tears from real crying but because she was so mad at herself. Acting like a stupid little kid, with no sense at all. There'd been those times—just a couple, a while back—he'd gone out, locked the door, *but the telephone had been right there*, and she just hadn't thought. Like a scared little kid, not using common sense the way Daddy Fred was always saying. Later on, when she'd wanted a telephone so bad— She still felt dim hatred for that apron man who'd stopped her going with Don— she'd thought about those times and hated herself.

And she was hungry, that was part of the hollow feeling, she knew, but they seemed to eat anything here but already cooked things brought in bags, the messy hamburgers in waxed paper, she liked hamburgers but not these, all red inside and too much mayonnaise and raw onion, and the fried chicken was all stiff and hard to chew.

Josie rolled over carefully on the old couch and looked out and down. It was a long way down to the street. All those stairs. It was hot in here, it looked hot and dusty out in the street. It wasn't a very different-looking street than Kingsley, except more apartments, not so many houses. There was one house far down the street she could just see part of, that looked like home, the same kind of house, with a long porch across the front.

Now she was thinking about it, she was awful hungry. She could think of a hundred things she'd like to eat right now, but it wasn't any use to ask Denny for one of them because they were all things only Mother Sue knew how to fix. Because of it being hot, first she thought about potato salad, all crisp and cold on lettuce, with things in it making it different from potato salad at school or anywhere else, and macaroni salad that wasn't quite as nice because of being slippery, and then she thought of just one tall glass of cold, cold milk, and she'd never wanted anything so bad—except the telephone. She could see it, almost touch it, the glass so cold, the milk rich and creamy and a little frothy on top—she licked her dry lips. The milk here didn't taste right even when it wasn't sour. She thought of cold meat loaf—they had it hot in winter, Mother Sue made it herself, with a lot of different things in it, hickory salt and flakes of parsley and little bits of red pepper, it was Daddy Fred's favorite—with hot cream gravy—and in summer sometimes they had it cold, sliced nice and thin, sometimes with gravy, sometimes with just mustard. And there were Jello salads Mother Sue made in summer—raspberry with pineapple inside, lime with all different kinds of fruit.

She looked out at the street, thinking dreamily about all the food, about the kitchen at home, the table all set for dinner, she always did that, and Bix always under the table and Mother Sue always saying, we should never have let him get in the habit of begging, and Daddy Fred saying, anything to make him happy. There were children down there playing in the street, mostly boys. She wondered, but not really concerned about it now, what would happen when school opened. People had to send children to school. But how would anyone find out if they didn't? Who knew Josie was here?

She knew—she didn't worry about that at all, it never entered her mind—that Mother Sue and Daddy Fred didn't know where she was. Or they'd have come after her and taken her home.

She tried to shut her mind to the blare of the TV out there, but she couldn't. When she got off the couch to go into the bathroom her legs felt weak and she had to hang onto the wash basin, but she got back to the couch and lay down again thankfully. Trying to draw a long breath, scared to try too long a breath, she choked just once, and lay very still, breathing shallowly, cautiously, afraid the nightmare would come again, but it didn't.

The next time she looked into the street, there was a woman up at the end of the driveway of the apartment across the street, waving and calling, and after a minute two children went running up the drive and in the back door there. The woman had been calling them in to dinner. Josie thought it was about that time.

The TV went on shouting out there. After a while it seemed to be fading away into a distance. Josie slept lightly, breathing shallow, slightly rasping little breaths.

◎◎◎

"Mr. Falkenstein," said Jean patiently, "you'll have to sign these depositions for the district attorney."

"What? Oh, yes." Jesse swiveled around in the desk chair and looked at her.

"And you said no appointments, but Mrs. Gorman called—she wants to add a codicil to her will—and there are four divorce hearings scheduled next week, I thought I'd remind you. A Mr. Galbraith called, you'd been recommended to him by Mrs. Cantwell, I said I'd call him back about an appointment. Do you feel all right, Mr. Falkenstein?"

"No," said Jesse. "Yes. Appointment—children—money. Yes, Jean. Next month that probate closes out, and all that damn loot is in common stock and I'll be damned if I know what kind of investment is safe any more but I'm not going to leave it in that. I wish to God I knew what he'd tell me to do with it. But—money—we've still got to earn a living, don't we, until comes the crash. Yes, all right, you call the man back and make an appointment. Tell Mrs. Gorman to come in Monday, the dear old soul. I'll sign those now."

"Are you sure you're all right, Mr. Falkenstein?" She was looking concerned.

"I am—" said Jesse, and stopped with his mouth open. "Oh, my God. Oh, my ears and whiskers. And I've got a signed, sealed and delivered degree in the practice of law—look at it, all prettily framed there under the clock. Oh, Edgar, how very right you are."

"Mr. Falkenstein," said Jean, alarmed, "what's wrong?"

"Me," said Jesse. "*The way of a fool is right in his own eyes,* so says Solomon. How very true. The rangers—going all around Robin Hood's barn—" He pulled himself together and focused on her, one of his two identical and very efficient secretaries, her pretty face wearing a frown at him. "After you've done that," he said, "I want you both to forget everything else and go down to the courthouse and look for a marriage license." Automatically she brought out pencil and notebook. "I don't know where it'd have been taken out, Orange County or L.A., but it should be on record downtown by now. Vincent Carson and bride. Probably two weeks to a month ago—

what with the blood tests they might have been foresighted about it. Better check back, any case, till you find it."

"Yes, Mr. Falkenstein. We'll get right on it."

◎◎◎

He came in the back door, that Friday night, and heard voices from the living room. After the smoggy humid heat outside, the dirty old streets, the traffic, air conditioning was welcome. There was a casserole of something in the oven, a tray of fresh-baked rolls under a napkin, a bowl of salad in the refrigerator. *"Whoso findeth a wife a good thing,* muttered Jesse, making straight for the ice-cube tray and getting down the bottle of Bourbon. He carried the drink into the living room. The baby was kicking and squirming on a blanket on the floor, and Nell and Fran were sitting there talking about ghosts.

"And you can say all you please about Borley Rectory," Fran was saying, "but I think that ghostly nun is a dead bore. Stereotyped. Good lord, Jesse—is it that late? I'd better get home—Andrew isn't convinced yet I'm the dedicated housewife, and if I don't have a meal ready when he gets home—"

"Preserve calm, I'm early," said Jesse. He sat down on the couch, stretched out his long legs and took a swallow of his drink. Athelstane attempted to climb into his lap, and the baby gurgled appreciation. "Quite right, I am due only derision. Not using the brains God gave me. You will both be interested to know that a marriage license was issued twelve days ago to Vincent Carson and Janet Mary Widmark, at the courthouse in Santa Ana. Her address was Anaheim."

"What?" said Fran.

"But that's—" Nell stared at him. "But it all fit in, Jesse! How could it—"

"All come apart? Very easy," said Jesse. "As I had the belated thought, girls. Coincidence does happen, all too frequently. Metropolitan area where six and a half million people live, and if the name Carson isn't as common as Sith, it's not all that unusual. Carson, Nonie said—likely off the top of her head—and so I went looking, playing the private eye, and against a million odds, so I thought, I dropped on a Carson and he'd just got married. Coincidence. Not really such long odds against it, you stop to think."

"But that's fantastic!" said Fran. "It just—throws it all back into limbo again. You don't know any more than you did at the beginning. But, Jesse—*why did she?*"

Jesse swallowed Bourbon and water. "Smart girl," he said, eyes shut. "You jumped there right away. Yes, why did she?"

"Look, I've got to run—I hope they'll have the power back on— It doesn't make any sense at all. Why should she have?"

"Try it," said Jesse, "on your trained-cop husband. He may not have taken any college courses in logic, but experience has taught him to reason from one to two to three." He had brought the bottle with him; he freshened his drink. "He'll tell you the one answer, Fran." He sounded quietly savage.

After she'd gone, Nell took the baby back to the nursery and folded the blanket. "Full circle," she said. "You're feeling mad about it—I don't blame you. That girl. Why did she, Jesse? Because I see that too."

"Why did she tell big sister that tale?" He sat up. "Oh, yes. Very likely the hastily made tale, the name produced on the spur of the moment—just bad luck it led off on a wild-goose chase. Why? It's no complex mystery. She was making an excuse to vanish for a while —it's the only answer, Nell. She kept in touch with big sister, Nonie —if she didn't, big sister would wonder, come poking around. So, the fairy tale—didn't big sister say it—to explain why Nonie wouldn't be around for a while."

"And why?" asked Nell blankly. "And why Josie?"

"I really don't know," said Jesse. "As my perspicacious little sister says, we're right back at the beginning."

He ate the casserole and salad disinterestedly. Nell, thinking about Nonie, was abstracted, herself. The baby had already been fed and was mercifully asleep, hopefully wouldn't get them up later. She stacked the dishes in the new dishwasher and went into the living room. He was sitting on the end of his spine in the recliner, staring at the Renoir print over the mantelpiece.

"You know," said Nell, "one thing in that tale rang true, Jesse. Nonie—she'd never had much. And trying to piece all this together, her dropping everything, leaving her job and moving so suddenly—

the only reason I can think of is, she saw a chance to get hold of some money. Mr. MacDonald said there was money concerned."

"There's no money anywhere in it," said Jesse. "They're all little people, ordinary people."

"But say there was, what would Josie have to do with it?"

"Nothing. No way."

Nell left him alone. He was feeling annoyed at being fooled by this little blond nonentity. But Nonie, by all they could guess, wasn't really very smart, was she? The scatterbrain, the flibbertigibbet.

When he came into the bedroom later on, she was sitting at the dressing table brushing and braiding her long hair for the night. She offered that opinion about Nonie, and he said yes, perfectly true. "But it's the child you can't help thinking about, isn't it, Jesse? We don't really know much about her, but she sounds like a nice little girl. The Lannings, nice people. Nonie—I don't know, between physical inheritance and environment, I always think environment's really more important. When you come to think about it—"

"Genes?" he said, and stood there with his tie in his hand, staring into space. "Josie. Well, she had two parents like everybody else, didn't she? Yes, indeed."

TEN

"Josie's father?" said Lanning. "Why, we never heard much at all, Mr. Falkenstein. As I told you, we never altogether believed that Nonie had been married. Now you say the mother's sure she was. But all she told us was that her husband had left her."

"Joe Johnson. Nothing about—oh, if he'd been working, where they were living then—"

"Not that I recall, no, nothing like that. Why?" asked Lanning.

"Just a point that came up. I'm wondering," said Jesse truthfully, "whether there was a divorce."

"Oh, I see. Well, I'm afraid I can't help you there."

Jesse put the phone down and said to himself sadly, "And why? 'Satiable curtiosity.'" But it was Saturday, no office hours; if he wanted to waste a little time it was his own business.

Before he got away from the house Fran arrived with Sally. "Because it's quite impossible, she chewed the nylon rope and got loose, and slipped the chain and got loose, and she's bitten all the men except the foreman. He understands Pekes."

"But Fran, you know Athelstane's terrified of her. He'll think we're going to keep her, the way it was before, and go right off his food, poor darling— You don't mean they're working on Saturday?"

"For a wonder, yes. It's just till five o'clock, Nell. You never saw such a mess, plaster and sawdust all over, and they've got the power off again. Andrew took one look at the new holes and said day off or not, the precinct house was more peaceful. And I'm meeting Jane for lunch at the Brown Derby and a nostalgic visit to the old office." Fran looked at Jesse. "I got there, by the way. Nonie wanted to disappear quietly. But what's Josie got to do with it?"

"At the moment, your guess is as good as mine."

Athelstane had taken one look at Sally and gone to skulk behind the recliner in the living room. Sally investigated his plate, finished his breakfast and sat licking her hairy chops. "Just until five," said Fran. "I'll pick her up."

"Honestly," said Nell. "Dogs!"

Jesse put on a tie and went out into another day of the expectable heat wave.

◎◎◎

"Well, I don't know why you'd be asking about him, all this time later," said Mrs. Brock. "Him and Nonie were just kids. I told her it was a fool thing, get married that young, sixteen she was and him just eighteen. At least she didn't have to get married, nothing like that. But you know girls that age—all romantic. In love. They get over that soon enough, have to think about where the rent's comin' from."

"Where did she meet him?" asked Jesse. "What was he like, Mrs. Brock? Was he in love with her?"

"I suppose he thought so, if that one ever was in love with anybody but himself." This time Jesse had penetrated to the front room of the house, and it was about what he'd expected. Old shabby furniture, everything neat but dreary, one picture on the long wall, a black and white reproduction of "The Return from the Tomb." She sat opposite him, fanning herself with a folded newspaper, wholly incurious as to why he was there. She said, "I got to be at work at ten-thirty. I hope the bus won't be late again. Meet him? Well, they were in school together, not either of them ever took much to school."

"Was he earning anything when they were married? Where did they live?"

"Oh, he had a job, at a garage around here, Riley's up on Hawthorne. But he wasn't makin' much, Nonie got a job in a drugstore, but then she got in the family way and couldn't work, sick as a dog she was, I told her how it'd be, but you can't talk to kids, can you? And that made Joe mad. She'd been payin' for his guitar lessons. He was a real selfish boy. Before long he just went off, and there she was, six months along and nowhere to go, and I took her in, of course."

"I see," said Jesse. "Did he come from around here? Family here?"

"We never knew his folks—his ma was widowed, I think, and I know she's dead now, a while ago I ran into that Browne woman on the bus and she mentioned it. I hadn't seen her in years, she's his aunt. You asked where they lived, well, she had a little apartment built on the back of her house and they rented that, but only four, five months. Gramercy Avenue it was. I always thought she was a downright mean woman, kick Nonie out right away after he left, but I guess selfishness runs in the family." She was rambling on at random. "What was he like? Just a kid, a long-haired kid thought he could play a guitar. Nonie was crazy about him, but after he left her like that, after a while she saw some sense like I'd tried to tell her, she never wanted to see him again, or I guess him her."

"I see. You never saw him again—she didn't hear from him?"

"No, nor wanted to. You still looking for her? She'll turn up somewheres," said Mrs. Brock.

Back in the car, Jesse debated. Ancient history: ten years back. The schools were closed, but the local school files wouldn't tell him anything about Nonie Brock, Joe Johnson, two nonentities of dropouts. He found a drugstore and a phone, looked for a Browne on Gramercy Avenue and for a wonder found one. He drove over there.

She was the prototype of every vinegarish spinster ever described: spare, upright, harsh-voiced, with suspicious eyes and a tight mouth. "Him?" she said, looking Jesse up and down. "I haven't seen Joe in years, can't say as I want to. Why?"

"I'm looking for the girl he was married to. Do you think—"

"Do I think he went back to her? I do not. Just like his father, but you couldn't tell my sister Millie a thing, last chance to get a man at thirty-five and him a bone-lazy bum, which she found out. Anyway, she's dead now, rest her soul. I haven't seen Joe in nearly ten years, and I couldn't have a guess where he'd be."

That was the kind of thing he could expect, of course, thought Jesse. Nonie and Joe both the drifters: little anonymous people. You could dig for records, but even in this age of appalling regimentation there wouldn't be many. Joe an eighteen-year-old kid, untrained for any job, probably as illiterate as Nonie, drifting around from one casual job to another.

And why he should be wasting time on this he didn't know.

He drove back to Hawthorne Boulevard and found Riley's garage: at least it said Riley's, whether or not it would be under the same management after ten years. There was only one car in the parking area in front, an old Cadillac; he left the Dodge beside it and walked into the oily-smelling cavern of the garage, where a rhythmic banging was going on. There was a little mild cussing at a dang-burned cold-stuck bolt, and then a man emerged from under the body of an old Mercury and said, "Do something for you?" He was a little gingery man with sharp eyes.

"Mr. Riley?"

"That's me. Selling something?"

"No. Looking for ancient history."

"Couldn't help you there, never was much of a student like they say."

"One Joe Johnson. You remember him at all? He used to work here."

"I wouldn't call it work," said Riley. "What in thunder you askin' about him for? Hadn't thought of him in years."

The regimentation was some use, offering excuses. "Social Security records," said Jesse. "Checking back."

"Oh. Come in and set down—I'm due a breather." In the tiny dirty office Riley offered him a cigarette. "Sure, I remember Joe. Him and my oldest son were buddies in school, and time he dropped out I had to talk to Bill like a Dutch uncle, get him to stay in till he graduated. Three, four years later he saw what I'd been talkin' about. Want to end up like that, I said, and he saw. Not that Joe was any worse than a lot I had in here, time to time. Not so much that they're lazy, these damn kids—never been taught how to do a good job of work at anything. Half the time goofing off like they say."

"Did you know the girl he married?"

"Nope. Think Bill did, sort of casual. It was when I heard he walked out on her I fired him. I could make excuses for a lot, and of course they was crazy to get married at all, just a pair of kids, but any man has any kind of spine don't walk off from responsibility, however tough the going is. I'd had enough of that one—*and* his family—by then. Him fooling around with a gee-tar half the time, pretending he could play the thing, and turning up at noon account he'd been rehearsing, he called it, with a bunch just like him. They used to play at night—night spots around here, for free, trying to get jobs. Well, I couldn't call to mind any names, except a place on Sepulveda, the Las Vegas Grill, it's still there, and Maudie's, everybody knows that one. But that was nine, ten years back, and I never seen him since. Listen, my records are all clear, I do all the books myself and there's never been any question—"

"His family?" said Jesse.

"Well, when I say that I meant that sister of his. There was a little bunch of kids used to run together some, my Bill, Joe, that Peggy Johnson, Moira Schultz, Tom Garner, Chuck Framingham—Joe was pretty struck with the Schultz girl awhile and then he up and married the other one. The Schultz girl and Tom Garner got married later and after he got out of the army they come back here and Tom works at the men's store right up the street. Small world. But that Peggy, she was bad medicine. Joe's sister. No better than she should be and then some, and for a while she was making a play at Bill, which I didn't like. A little tramp by the time she was fifteen. But I get to talking, you were askin' about Joe. I never laid eyes on him since, and I got no idea where he is or what doing. But like I say, my records are all straight, and besides that's a hell of a long time ago."

Jesse agreed that it was, thanked him, backed the Dodge out. Just where he thought he was going on this— He found the men's store in the next block, parked and went in and looked over some cheap sports coats. There was only one clerk in the place, a man about the right age. "You Mr. Garner? I've just been talking to Mr. Riley down the street. Understand you used to know a Joe Johnson, went to school with him."

"Why, that's right. I'll be damned, hadn't thought of Joe in years," said Garner amiably. "You a friend of his?"

"Friend of a friend," said Jesse vaguely.

"Well, I'll be damned, how's old Joe doing these days? Now this is our newest line, and very good value for the money, if you'd like to try one on— Funny, when you look back, the crazy notions kids get. Joe was hot to get into show business, him and a couple others got up a little combo, he had me all fired up about it, I used to fool around with the sax. But it's no way to earn a living. What's he doing these days?"

"He didn't say," said Jesse. "Sorry, I don't see just what I'm looking for."

He sat in the Dodge and smoked a cigarette, finally found another phone book and looked up the addresses: the Las Vegas Grill and Maudie's. He tried the grill first. It was an old building newly refronted with smart white brick, and looked like a fairly classy place; it was just open at noon. He went in, asked the first waitress he saw for the proprietor and was admitted, on sending in a card, to a small masculine office past the twin rest rooms.

"If it's a damage suit of any kind, I'm covered six ways from Sunday by insurance," said the proprietor, giving him a hard stare. "Ferguson's the name. Is it?"

"No. Trying to trace somebody," said Jesse. "Have you owned the place long?"

"Ever since it's been here, twelve years. Who?" Ferguson was a beefy fellow, very businesslike.

"Recall hiring a combo of young musicians, about nine, ten years back? One of them a Joe Johnson? It's possible they offered to play for nothing, get experience."

"Mister, are you kidding?" Ferguson laughed. "When I was building up trade, that long ago, I must've had fifty lousy little combos offer to play in here—punk kids with the idea it's an easy way to make a buck. Joe Johnson? Now who the hell would remember a Joe Johnson for ten minutes? I never did much like the idea of feeding people music with their food, and the kind of thing passes for music nowadays, apt to give 'em indigestion. I let a few of those kids in here, few times in the early days, but not since. It's strictly good food and service these days, and no way would I remember any of those horn blowers now, sorry."

Jesse got back in the Dodge and went to the other place, on 190th Street. Maudie's was a very different proposition from the Las Vegas Grill. It was in the middle of an old block, an ancient brick building. It had double front doors, and what looked like a hand-painted sign on a bracket over them: in tremulous curlicues and much-renewed poster paint it said MAUDIE'S YOUR FAVORITE REST STOP. There was another hand-lettered sign inside one front window that said NO FREE LUNCH BUT THE 75¢ ONE'S GOOD. A third sign, temporary by

comparison, was tacked to the right-hand front door; it said in strag-
gly printing BACK TO OPEN 4:30—CAR ON FRITZ.

What was called a character, decided Jesse. He didn't feel any pas-
sionate enthusiasm to meet Maudie. He got back in the Dodge and
drove home.

And what the hell did it matter now, what kind Joe Johnson had
been, what he'd done, or where he was now? It was just another
loose end, and a long way from the middle of the tangle. From the
little he did know about this, it was doubtful that Joe and Nonie
would ever have got together again, and it was Nonie he was interested in.

In any case, he didn't know for certain that there hadn't been a divorce. After his lack of brilliance over the Carson marriage license,
that was one loose end he should tie up; and he couldn't get into the
courthouse until Monday. Of course, Johnson could have got a divorce anywhere else, and it needn't be in L.A.'s records. But just to
tidy up as he went along—

Went along where? Nowhere. Where the hell had the girl gone,
why had she told that tale and why had she taken Josie? Money.
There wasn't any smell of money, anywhere all this had led him, except Carson, and Carson didn't have one damn thing to do with
Nonie. Carson was a big fat coincidence.

Which he hadn't yet told the Lannings. Which he had better do.
And it was all he could tell them, damn it.

Danger to the child.

And he couldn't say that he was at all worried about Nonie—
wherever she was, for whatever reason: Nonie could take care of herself, after a fashion. But where was Josie, snatched away from home
by the stranger?

◎◎◎

There was just not one more lead to chase down, and it was use-
less to go on thinking about it, but that didn't stop him, of course.

When he broke the news to the Lannings, they were very quiet,
she grave and he grim. Lanning said to him, "If I borrowed on the
house—I could probably get ten thousand—would it be any use to
hire a private detective?"

Jesse didn't know what to tell him. If a professional could ferret out another link to Nonie, he didn't know how or where.

Nell said she was going mad with Athelstane peering around corners at Sally and Sally leaving hair all over the furniture. And Fran was an even better housekeeper, she probably complained about the hair too, but of course Andrew was besotted over that dog.

"Yes," said Jesse. "Very accomplished burglar chaser, our Sally." He went into the den and stacked Bach on the phonograph. Nell got on with her book, one ear cocked for the baby.

But at four-thirty Jesse suddenly emerged, the phonograph stilled, and put on his tie again.

"Call it obstinacy, or damn foolishness. I won't get anything there either. But at least I could say I'd looked in every last single hole. And hole's the word. I'll tell you about it later."

◎◎◎

She was a character. A big, hearty, raddled woman with violently hennaed hair, purple lipstick and nail polish, a black satin dress strained across a generous bosom. But there was essential good sense and good nature about Maudie, a humorous earthy acceptance of the world of people for what it was. She had only a few customers in at this hour, and she sat at a table with Jesse and offered him a beer, which he declined.

"I don't want to take up your time. You're alone here?" No barkeep behind the bar.

"Hire any help, it eats up profits," she said, showing a couple of gold teeth. "Don't fuss about the customers, all regulars and I've got 'em trained to wait on themselves and chalk it up honest. What can I do for a lawyer?"

At least he didn't have to make up a story for her: she would take it for granted that everybody was as interested in people as she was, and not wonder why he was asking. He thought suddenly that the old man would have enjoyed her immensely.

"Oh, sure, I remember the Johnsons," she said. "Him I didn't know like I knew her, but I knew 'em both. Poor damn kids, learning about life the hard way. Thinking the fairy tale's gonna come true just for wishing. That Joe, the others, gonna break in show business and make a million—break their hearts at it, and end up fifth-rate honky-tonks, or takin' honest jobs if they was lucky—and smart. Which I wouldn't say any of 'em was. I never heard what happened to Joe later on, last time I knew he was workin' part time at a car wash somewhere around, for eating money and guitar lessons. Her, I know where she ended up, that fool broad."

"Nonie?" asked Jesse sharply.

"Who's Nonie? I'm talkin' about Peggy—Joe's sister. I sized her up first time I saw her, come in here with Joe. She was makin' it with one of the other guys in the combo, but not long. Her kind, they can't stay with anything long—men, jobs, places. Sometimes they make out all right, even so, but mostly they don't. She didn't."

"What happened to her?"

Maudie had been chain-smoking; she coughed and spat out a tobacco shred. "She got busted first for the soliciting bit, tried some of that in here but I wasn't havin' any. I dunno how many times she was picked up. Got so she couldn't make bail. Then she got on the booze, and finally the dope. She passed out in the General Hospital three, four years back, and I don't guess by then there was anybody to go to her funeral. I often wondered if they came down on Joe to pay for it, he'd be mad as blazes, tight-fisted like he was. She didn't have no other relations I know of."

"There's an aunt," said Jesse, "but from what I've heard, she and Joe are a pair."

⊚⊚⊚

"But that's just nothing," said Nell.

"Nothing at all," agreed Jesse.

The baby got them up at two o'clock, and after getting back to sleep at four Jesse stayed in bed on Sunday morning. He got up and into a bathrobe at eleven o'clock, looked at the paper for five minutes, switched on the news for the weather and grunted when the forecaster said brightly, continued heat and smog. Five minutes later he sat up, went down the hall and picked up the phone. Athelstane, still somewhat subdued after a day of Sally, slunk after him.

"Excuse the interruption, Andrew. Do something for me?"

"Now what?"

"Ask your Records about Joe Johnson. He ever picked up for anything? If so what?"

"Would you like to guess how many Joe Johnsons there'll be in our files?"

"Pick the right one by dates. He'd be eighteen ten years ago, probable address Torrance. His sister Peggy's in your records, prostitution and narco."

"Oh, really. Well, we've got computers too," said Clock. "I'll put it through and get back to you. Though where this wild goose is leading you—"

Half an hour later he called back. "He was there. I think the right one, the dates match. Six-one, a hundred and eighty, black and blue, no marks. He was picked up for possession as a J.D., then auto theft four times, one assault and a felony hit-run, which is why he's in our records. He got a one-to-three on that, served eight months and went out on P.A. Nothing heard of him since his parole ended."

"Oh." Jesse digested that. "Could you get me the name of his parole officer?"

"I've got nothing to do but chase down information for you, of course. I'll see who's in at Welfare and Rehab." But Clock didn't call back after that until nearly three o'clock. "Sorry, Jesse, we had that damn sniper on the freeway again. I hope he's not going to make it a habit every Sunday. Johnson's P.A. officer was a Clarence Chantry. He's retired since last year, but I got his address—the fellow I talked to knows him. He's living with a married daughter in Hidden Hills. Hoback Canyon Road."

"I am getting around these days," said Jesse. "Thanks, Andrew."

Hidden Hills was out toward the end of the valley, hotter than Hollywood, and the Sunday traffic was thick. By the time he got where he was going, Jesse's eyes were smarting from the smog and he was asking himself again what the hell he thought he was doing. Conscientious lawyer, chasing down loose ends. Bemused by the secondhand report of a middling good clairvoyant. Led on more by what MacDonald had said.

Surprisingly, for this newly grown-up community, it was an old house tucked away on a big lot at the end of a winding road, nearly hidden by dense trees. A comfortable-looking middle-aged woman opened the door to him.

"Dad? Why, he'll be pleased for any company, especially from the force, you said? It was past time he retired, but he hasn't much to keep him occupied these days. Come right in." She led him through a dim living room to a little square den where an old man sat reading a magazine. There was a room air conditioner in here, steadily whirring.

Mr. Chantry was pleased to see a new face. He was a tall, spare old man with a bald head, and he fussed over Jesse, picking just the right chair, calling on his daughter for lemonade, eager to talk on any subject. The one Jesse offered him pleased him even more.

"Well, it's very funny you should be asking about him, Mr. Falkenstein. I know there's a lot of bitter talk about the parole system, and there's no question but that the board's too lenient nowadays. But I always tried to do my best as a conscientious officer, especially with the young ones. You needn't tell me, rehabilitation just a joke with all too many of them. But just once in a while, I'd feel that I'd really accomplished something. That one was a case in point.

"Of course, he hadn't a long or very bad record. But he'd been on the marijuana, which is all to often the first step on the way down— all the way down. He was interested in music, and I managed to find him a job at a recording studio, just carrying the props, but it was a little contact for him. When his parole ended, he'd joined a country western group. Makes you wonder about fate," said Chantry chattily. "To think of him getting where he is today, just from that little encouragement. Or maybe he would have anyway. But—"

"Where he is today?" echoed Jesse.

"Why, yes. I recognized him right away, when I first saw a picture. Not that I'm a film fan, or listen to modern music either—not much music about it, ask me, and I can't see talent enters into it. All the same, there he is at the top, when he might have ended up just another junkie running the streets. It's a mystery to me why a fellow like that can get paid a hundred grand a year for caterwauling not much different from my teen-age grandson, but—"

"Who is he?" asked Jesse loudly.

"Why, this new star, Vic O'Neal—I suppose they'd have to give him a new name, Joe Johnson not very inspired," and Chantry laughed. "I recognized his picture right away when I first noticed it, him in some TV show just this season, and a couple of movies too."

"I will be damned," said Jesse. "I will be damned!"

"Luck or talent or whatever," said Chantry, "seems peculiar to think that ordinary junkie with a little pedigree's now up there making a bundle and hobnobbing with a lot of millionaires and TV stars —should think he'd have a lot to learn, how to act with a crowd like that, formal manners and—"

Jesse leaped to his feet and dropped the glass of lemonade all over the rug. "*Ambassaors!*" he exclaimed wildly. "A rose by any other— *Ambassadors!* New York—*New York!* Oh, my God! Oh, my God!" And he turned and ran for the door. Chantry looked after him with his mouth open.

He fell into the Dodge, nearly flooded the engine, got it started and made back for the freeway fast. A kaleidoscope of small thoughts chased across his mind, he still didn't know what the hell this meant, but two things he saw, or thought he saw—

"But she didn't have to tell that tale!" he said aloud. "Get *out* of the way, damn you— She didn't have to at all, because— Drive it or park it! Oh, hell, I'll never make that signal— New York! The dignitaries—ambassadors!"

There was a pile-up on the freeway just before the Laurel Canyon exit; he sat and fumed while the squard cars passed, and ambulance, eventually the tow trucks. It was six-twenty when they let traffic proceed, and Nell would be wondering where he was, probably worrying; he couldn't help it. He went straight down Western to Adams, cursing the signals, the traffic, turned there and slowed for the side streets, looking at signs—he'd been here only once before.

Manhattan; and it was the old four-story building in the middle of the block. He slid the Dodge into a yellow zone, leaped out and ran in the front door, took the stairs three at a time.

There was a man standing in front of the apartment door, a slim fortyish man with blond hair, dressed in too-fancy sports clothes. His finger was still on the bell. Jesse came up behind him in a rush as the door opened, and the man spun around, startled; but Jesse was looking beyond him.

"Where's Josie, Mrs. Lefkowitz?" he asked, and her expression froze as she saw him there. For just an instant the little tableau held; them she screamed out one obscenity and tried to slam the door, but he held it and pushed her back into the room. "Where's Josie, Mrs. Lefkowitz?"

"I came to see a Mrs. Johnson, baby," said the other man. "And who're you, friend?"

"Goddamn all of you!" she said, and suddenly she collapsed onto the couch and began to cry weakly, rocking back and forth. "Only chance I ever had—any money—not even hurt anybody to get it— only chance I ever would have—and it all went wrong, everything going wrong—"

Jesse left her without a glance and loped down a narrow hall to one bedroom—empty: back to another, dim-lighted. Something on the couch—he found a lamp, and there was Josie. She looked very thin and small, hunched up there, and her eyes were imploring, and her breath came in hard, choking gasps.

He ran back to the living room, put in a call to the paramedics and then to Wilcox Street. He said to the other man, "I think we let the cops sort this out. Where's Nonie, Mrs. Lefkowitz?"

She raised dull eyes to his, and now she looked almost indifferent. "Nonie's dead," she said. "She's dead."

Clock had been kept late in the office, waiting for a long-distance call, and was just leaving when Jesse came in with the pair of them, the uniformed men from the Traffic unit. The night watch wasn't on yet, so they were alone in the big detective office, at first only Clock and Jesse sitting in, later some of the men from the night watch. She told them about Denny, and Clock sent a Traffic unit to pick him up, sitting in at a hand of gin at Lew's bar.

"That goddamned stupid bastard," she said, "it was him made most of the trouble, he's not going to get out of anything! If he hadn't killed that other bastard—"

His name turned out to be Denny Carson—so that was where the coincidental Carson had come from—and he had a pedigree: assault, armed robbery. He was very surprised to be pulled in; he looked at her in bewilderment and said, "But we were goin' to get the payoff! Everything was goin' to be O.K.! What went wrong, for God's sake?"

"Had to bring this damn shyster into it—" Christine was huddled in the chair beside Clock's desk. "Somebody for God's sake give me a cigarette. Those goddamned people had the kid! All going wrong. How could I know they wouldn't be glad to get rid of the kid? The payoff was getting set up—"

"From you?" said Clock to the other man, who had just trailed along, watchful. Now he reached into his breast pocket and handed Clock a card.

"For my sins, getting into this business. And now this mess."

"Mr. Steve Quiller. Theatrical agent. Where do you come in?"

"In the final scene, baby. I think."

"Suppose we hear about Nonie," said Jesse. "She's dead. How?"

Christine drew on the cigarette. "It's all shot to hell, I might as well tell you," she said drearily. "You'd get it all out of Denny anyway. It all started with that bum she married. Joe. I hadn't thought of the guy in years and neither had she, and then I saw this story in that sheet, the *National Questioner*, you know the one. I don't go to movies, watch much TV, I'd heard the name, big new star, but I hadn't seen a picture of him before. And it was Joe. Joe! That crummy kid she'd married back there. Right on top and all that money—the story said, fifty G's for a TV appearance, and making a movie now, quarter of a million. Joe! I got hold of Nonie, showed it to her, I said look, she was due some of that money. For herself and the kid—he never even saw the kid, gave her one dime for support. And she was going to get some—she was all excited about it, wouldn't she be? She'd never seen a picture before either, but she knew him right away. I said to her, better do it right, all legal, get a lawyer. And better not say anything to anybody till it all goes through. For once she listened to me. She didn't tell anybody else, nobody knew but me and him—" She nodded at Denny.

"Boy friend?" said Clock.

"And I should've had my head examined, take up with him!"

"Aw, now, spit-cat," said Denny weakly.

"And then she had to tell him. Her guy. McAllister. Sure we knew him, we went out together sometimes. And that was the first thing happened," said Chris drearily. "It was just the day after, my God. He came and told us she was dead. Nonie. He was all to pieces, and I didn't blame him. My God, what a break! They'd gone someplace to a party that night and there was dope floating around and Nonie got some. She'd never gone on that kick, but she was feeling excited that night—to think of all the money coming—and she took some, or got fed some, I don't know. Maybe she had a weak heart or something, I don't know that either, but God, what a break! She was out cold, McAllister said, and he got her in the car, but when he got to her apartment she was—but cold. Dead. He was scared. He kept saying, he wasn't about to get tied into a homicide, that's what you'd call it. He didn't know what to do, he was afraid to carry her into the place, there was a party going on, people coming and going. He drove around some, he said, trying to think what to do, and it was starting to get light and he just drove up in the park a ways and put her under some bushes. Up above Outpost somewhere, he said."

Cock let out a breath. "Somewhere in Wattles Garden Park."

"I guess. Did you find her?"

"Oh, we found her," said Clock. "So that was Nonie. I see."

"Listen, it was an awful shock. My kid sister. Not that we were so awfully close—"

"No, I saw that, belatedly," said Jesse. "She wouldn't really have bothered to tell you that elaborate tale, as an excuse to vanish. She'd just have gone, and let you wonder a little."

"Listen, it was awful—but—I mean, God, the chance at all that money, all down the drain. He'd have to pay up, on account of the kid. We'd talked about it—she'd have to get the kid back, of course, awhile anyway—get the lawyer—it was then she'd told me where the kid was, I didn't know before. Just thinking about all that money— And that damn McAllister knew! He said right then maybe we could still get it. That I—"

"Looked like Nonie," said Jesse softly. "Older, but you looked like her. Could you have fooled Joe?"

She shrugged impatiently. "I knew he wouldn't want to see Nonie or the kid. He'd just have to pay up. But—if I tried it—we couldn't do it exactly that way, all level. It'd have to be under the counter, sort of. But he owed something for the kid, didn't he? See, that story in the paper, it had the name of his agent too. This Mr. Quiller. It said, clever young public relations man. And I thought, Do it through him—Joe's his property, kind of, to protect. His ten per cent of the loot."

"How true," murmured Quiller.

"And, damn it, McAllister had to know—he'd want a cut, and I wasn't about to give him one! I told him I couldn't do that. But Denny and I went to Nonie's place, and he used a shim to get us in, and I cleared everything out, make it look like she'd moved. And I saw I'd have to get the kid. The rest of it I had to have—Nonie hadn't kept any of that—it was easy. The birth certificate once, when I applied at Lockheed. I just went down to the courthouse and asked, they give you copies for three bucks. But I had to have the kid, because even doing it under the counter, somebody—this agent —'d want to see her, see she was alive. You can see that." She put out her cigarette, lit another nervously. "How the hell did I know she was going to be a—as big a kid—my God, time gets away from you, I'd forgot how long—"

"Not very big," said Jesse.

"And how the hell did I know those people wouldn't be glad to get rid of her?" She looked at Jesse in helpless fury. "Had to bring *you* into it! And then this Quiller saying he couldn't get in touch with Joe—"

"Well, I couldn't," said Quiller. "He's been on location, some mountain village in Spain, no cablegrams. I ask you. I wasn't about to pay off this dame and take a chance on his paying me back— Vicky boy I know, miser from way back, that one. Sure, he'd have to pay up, and better do it quiet. Relaxed morals these days, friends, wouldn't make the stink it might once, his deserting girl-wife and chee-ild, but I thought it was only fair, once we were sure it was on the level. My secretary went and had a look at the papers—"

"And that one's on the make if I know anything," said Chris viciously.

"You may be right, doll. Thought it all looked kosher, but didn't like you so good, baby."

"I'll bet!" said Chris. "And then, damn it, McAllister had to come nosing around—he probably suspected I was going to try for it—he

walked in on Denny and that damn fool had to open his mouth—
And he wanted a cut, and I wasn't about to— But this goddamn
idiot Denny—"

"Aw, listen," said Denny. He looked nearly ready to cry. "I didn't
mean to do a thing like that, I told you."

"Saying you'd take care of him! Don't worry, you'd chase him off!
Brother, you did, but good! I—"

"I never meant to kill the guy," said Denny hurriedly, anxious to
explain to Clock. "Just rough him up a little bit, let him know he
wasn't going to get nothing. Come to think, he was the one, he took
Nonie wherever it was she got the dope. It was kind of all his fault,
come to think—"

Jesse met Clock's eyes. The stupid little people.

"When you told me, I nearly died!" said Christine to Jesse. "A
murder. This stupid bastard, I knew it was him did it, and no telling
if he'd left his prints plastered all over—"

"Aw, kitten, I know better than that."

"And I saw then"—she was still looking at Jesse—"you'd never be
satisfied till you found Nonie. Or thought you knew where she was. I
had to stop you nosing around—until after the pay off, just till then.
Quiller stalling and stalling—and a murder, the cops mixed in—I
had to put you off, some way, to stop you hunting for Nonie, till we
got the payoff."

"It was a nice story," said Jesse. "I scared you, hinting it might be
a lie right away."

She uttered a half sob. "Ten years off my life. I just tried to pass it
off—like I thought so too. And Quiller stalling some more—"

"I'd got to thinking I wanted to have a look for myself," said
Quiller. "Reason I was calling on the lady, date set up. I got through
to Vic yesterday, and he was mad as hell—never expected to hear
from the girl-wife again, I gather. He hadn't mentioned her to me."

"And what," asked Jesse, "had you planned to do with Josie after
the payoff? Or had you got that far?"

"Oh, for God's sake," she said, "what do I know about kids? That
was the only thing besides the money that looked good to me right
then—these people wanted the kid back, you said. So they could
have her. I never meant any harm to the kid, for God's sake. She had

that awful attack, we got her the medicine. She was picky about eating, but for God's sake, nobody starved her."

"No," said Jesse. He laughed. "You could call it a comedy of errors, couldn't you?"

"Except," said Clock, "for the homicides. There'll be statements for you to sign—all of you. I'll be applying for warrants on you and Denny, Mrs. Lefkowitz. Right now we'll send you both to jail."

And Denny said unexpectedly, "Is the kid all right, Sergeant? She's a nice little kid." He was no stranger to jail; that didn't move him.

It would be a new experience for Chris. She looked at Jesse with dull resentment; she said, "They had to bring you into it!"

◎◎◎

"Little mess," said Quiller, on his feet. "I suppose Vic gets drawn in, some way. As the motive. What'll the charges be?"

Clock shrugged. "Depends how far the D.A. wants to go. Fraud, possibly kidnapping, though that's borderline—she is the child's aunt. Fraud at least."

"Oh. I'm not offering a bribe."

"I should hope not," said Clock.

"But he sure as hell does owe something, for the kid. He'll kick like a bay steer, but I'll persuade him. The good publicity. He lost track of wife and chee-ild, hunted all over, frantic to share good fortune and now he'll make the magnificent settlement. I suppose these people do want the child back? Well, there'll be a payoff. The things that happen in this business," and he went out, walking lithely.

One of the detectives on the night watch had taken Chris and Denny jailward. Jesse had called Nell when he first landed there, so she wouldn't be worrying. He hoped she wasn't up with the baby. He realized suddenly that he was starving; it was a quarter to midnight.

"Well, it's always nice to get all the answers," said Clock. "To think of all my deductions on McAllister—isn't it simple when you know."

Jesse was dialing. He got handed around a little, eventually talked

H 03

to a nurse who told him that Josie was fine. She'd eaten a good supper and was sound asleep, she could go home tomorrow. "I had better," said Jesse to Clock, "call the Lannings."

Clock yawned. "The girls'll be interested to know how it came out. I hope to God they'll finish installing the air conditioning tomorrow. My God, Jesse, you can't call them now—it's nearly midnight."

Jesse grinned at him. Against all the odds, it had all come out all right. And he had the warm conviction—damn the evidence, what kind or how it came—that the old man was still there. Just the same as always, not very far away at all, only in dimension instead of space.

"You know, Andrew," he said, "I don't really think the Lannings will mind being waked up."